# TYPEWRITER
# IN THE SKY

# Among the Many Classic Works
## by L. Ron Hubbard

The Automagic Horse

Battlefield Earth

The Beast

Buckskin Brigades

The Case of the Friendly Corpse

The Dangerous Dimension

Death's Deputy

Fear

Final Blackout

The Ghoul

The Indigestible Triton

The Invaders

The Kilkenny Cats Series

Kingslayer

The Mission Earth Dekalogy*

Volume 1: The Invaders Plan

Volume 2: Black Genesis

Volume 3: The Enemy Within

Volume 4: An Alien Affair

Volume 5: Fortune of Fear

Volume 6: Death Quest

Volume 7: Voyage of Vengeance

Volume 8: Disaster

Volume 9: Villainy Victorious

Volume 10: The Doomed Planet

Ole Doc Methuselah

Slaves of Sleep

& The Masters of Sleep

To the Stars (a.k.a. Return to Tomorrow)

Tough Old Man

The Tramp

The Ultimate Adventure

*Dekalogy: a group of ten volumes

# Typewriter in the Sky

## L. Ron Hubbard

BRIDGE PUBLICATIONS, INC., LOS ANGELES

ISBN 0-88404-933-7

# INTRODUCTION

It had been a horrendous six months.

I had written a 500-page "Star Wars" novel (from start to finish in eight weeks), then moved right into an ambitious science fiction novel, the most complex book I had ever attempted (also 500 pages, also done in about two months), then I completed the third novel in a Young Adult series co-written with my wife, and then there were the juvenile science fiction books, the editing of three anthologies, writing comic book scripts, a few short stories . . . Don't expect me to keep track of it all.

And here I had always imagined being an author simply entailed wearing cable-knit sweaters and dangling an unlit pipe from one corner of the mouth, all the while waiting to be inspired by the elusive Muse . . .

Which was why, when the phone rang—the twelfth time that day—I was somewhat daunted by the conversation. It was my friend from Bridge Publications, and he wanted me to write the introduction for a reprint of L. Ron Hubbard's classic novel "Typewriter in the Sky."

I finally got him off the phone by saying, "Just send me a copy of the book, and I'll read it. If I like it, I might be able to write you something. When is the absolute latest I can turn in the introduction?"

The book arrived before I managed to forget what I had promised, and so I hefted it in my hand, cocked my arm back, and tossed it to the top of my stack of things to read. That evening, as I attempted to dissolve in a hot bath, I leaned back and flipped to page one of "Typewriter in the Sky" and began to read:

—about a harried writer behind on his deadlines, buried under dozens of projects, and talking as fast as he can to convince his editor that everything is indeed under control, that the blockbuster novel (which he hasn't even started yet) is well on its way.

*Boy, things sure haven't changed in fifty years!*

Right away I knew I was going to enjoy reading this book. Very much, in fact.

"Typewriter in the Sky" is about Mike de Wolf, friend of the popular pulp fiction writer Horace Hackett, who—through a freak accident—finds himself transported into the pages of Hackett's swashbuckling work-in-progress . . . and to his horror finds himself cast as the villain!

Mike, having read most of his friend's hack fiction, knows full well what a horrible end Horace's villains *always* encounter!

Since the original publication of this novel, Mr. Hubbard's idea has often been emulated. As "The New Encyclopedia of Science Fiction," edited by James Gunn (1988) says, "Typewriter in the Sky, which anticipates plot gimmicks now popular among experimental metafictionists, ought to be taken seriously by the critics who will evaluate his strange genius." Author Frederik Pohl said much the same: "Fans and other writers were doing variations on that for years." Most recently, John Carpenter's film *In the Mouth of Madness* adds a macabre twist to this idea: horror novelist Sutter Cane has such power in his prose that he was able to rewrite the world according to his own nightmarish visions.

"Typewriter in the Sky," though, is a much more exhilarating romp, filled with delightful twists and turns. Mr. Hubbard uses the material to its fullest effect, playing even self-parody to great effect. The snapshots of the New York writing life in the 1940s are pure gems.

The tale of a modern man stranded in a pirate adventure, complete with obvious anachronisms and sloppy details, makes the reader's head spin. Mike de Wolf comments aloud about his own stilted dialog, how his surroundings blatantly change as the writer pounding on his "typewriter in the sky" remembers belatedly to put in the necessary details.

Once he finally figures out what has happened, Mike must play upon the predictability of Horace's hackneyed plots to save himself and change the outcome of the story. Meanwhile, outside the story, Horace Hackett himself goes to a bar to commiserate with another pulp fiction writer about how sometimes characters just sort of take on lives of their own! "Typewriter in the Sky" is a true masterpiece of the genre, my personal favorite among the L. Ron Hubbard books I have read.

This novel was published in two installments in the November and December 1940 issues of *Unknown* magazine by the famous science fiction editor, John W. Campbell, Jr. The author had had an intensely productive year in 1940, and "Typewriter in the Sky" was written under great pressure—but L. Ron Hubbard seemed to work well under pressure.

That same year, within a six-month span, he produced two more of his greatest works, the chilling psychological horror novel "Fear" (soon to be a major motion picture) and the bleak story of the aftermath of a future war, "Final Blackout." (And only months earlier, in July 1939, one of his other favorites, "Slaves of Sleep," was published in *Unknown* magazine.) In short, it was a very good year for vintage L. Ron Hubbard.

At his peak, Mr. Hubbard was astoundingly prolific, publishing 154 novels and short stories—over ten million words—in the decade from 1930 to 1940. With the low pay rates of the day, pulp fiction writers were forced to be prolific or starve—and there was absolutely no question of L. Ron Hubbard starving! He supposedly wrote a hundred words a minute on an electric typewriter on many diverse topics. Following the credo that "a writer writes," Mr. Hubbard was indeed a **writer**.

He follows a tradition set by a number of classic authors who wrote quickly and in first-draft form. Alexandre Dumas, Jules Verne and Charles Dickens were amazingly prolific, and their works have remained on bookshelves for more than a century. Dickens wrote "A Christmas Carol," one of the best-loved novels of all time, in a feverish frenzy that lasted only a few days. William Faulkner supposedly wrote his classic "As I Lay Dying" in one weekend and published his first draft without a single editorial change.

L. Ron Hubbard was a very different type of writer from the one-book-per-decade "artistes" whose work was wrenched out with angst and hair-pulling to critical acclaim (one hopes), yet was totally devoid of enjoyment.

"Typewriter in the Sky," as I discovered, is a book that remembers how to be *fun* and entertaining, a pleasure to read instead of a chore.

Sit back, relax, and enjoy the ride!

**—Kevin J. Anderson**

# CHAPTER ONE

Horace Hackett, as one of his gangster characters would have said, was on the spot. About three months before, Jules Montcalm of Vider Press had handed to Horace Hackett the sum of five hundred dollars, an advance against royalties of a novel proposed but not yet composed. And Horace Hackett, being an author, had gaily spent the five hundred and now had nothing but a hangover to present to Jules Montcalm. It was, as one of Horace Hackett's heroes would have said, a nasty state of affairs. For be it known, publishers, when they have advanced sums against the writing of a book, are in no mood for quibbling, particularly when said book is listed in the fall catalogue and as there were just two months left in which it could be presented to the public.

Horace Hackett was popular, but not popular enough to get away with anything like that. He wrote novels of melodramatic adventure for Vider Press, at about the rate of one a year—though he also wrote gang stories for Pubble House and love stories for Duffin & Co. Just now Horace Hackett was furiously fumbling with facts in an attempt to explain to Jules Montcalm just why it was that no manuscript had arrived as per contract. Jules Montcalm, being a publisher, did not believe authors. In fact, it is doubtful if Jules Montcalm ever believed anything beyond the fact that he was probably the one genius in the book business. He had, let us say, a suspicious eye. This he had focused upon Horace Hackett and Horace Hackett squirmed.

They were in the living room of Horace Hackett's Greenwich Village basement studio apartment, a darkish place well padded with sheets of forgotten manuscripts, unanswered letters from bill collectors, notes from the ex-wife's lawyer asking for alimony, empty brandy bottles, broken pencils, a saddle somebody had sent from New Mexico, several prints of furious revolutionary battles, three covers from some of Horace's magazine serials, crumpled packages of cigarettes—all empty—a stack of plays somebody had sent—just knowing that Horace could advise about them—newspapers which dated back to the tenth battleship Germany had claimed to have sunk, a number of scatter rugs from Colombia, where they had begun life as saddle pads, three empty siphons, a dun from the company which had foolishly financed Horace Hackett's car and a piano at which sat Michael de Wolf.

Horace Hackett did not appear disturbed. In fact, he was airy. This thing, his attitude plainly said, was a mere bagatelle. Why, the business of dashing off that novel was so simple and could be done so quickly that one wondered why another one should think twice about it. But deep down, under his soiled bathrobe, Horace Hackett knew that he had never been closer to getting caught.

Mike de Wolf, at the piano, was grandly oblivious of the pair. His slender fingers were caressing a doleful dirge from the stained keys, a very quiet accompaniment to his own state of mind. Mike had a chance to audition the following morning, but he was pretty certain that he would fail. He always had, hadn't he?

Jules Montcalm, with the air of a hunter who has just treed a mountain lion and is now training his rifle to bop it out of the branches, leveled a finger at Horace.

"I don't believe," said Jules Montcalm—whose real name was Julius Berkowitz—"that you even have a plot for it!"

"Heh, heh, heh," said Horace, hollowly. "Not even a plot. Heh, heh. That is very funny. Mike, he doesn't even think I've got a plot for this novel!"

"Well," said Mike de Wolf, not turning, "have you?" And he ran into a more mournful set of chords than before.

"Heh, heh. You don't think for a minute that Mike means that, do you, Jules? Why, of course I've got a plot!"

"Uh-huh," said Jules. "I bet you can't even begin to tell me about that plot!"

"Here, have another drink," said Horace, getting hurriedly up and pulling his dirty bathrobe about him while he poured Jules another drink.

"Well, if you got a plot, then why don't you tell it to me and stop saying 'Heh, heh, heh!' " Jules had scored.

Horace sat in the chair, still airy, and he managed to put an enthusiastic light behind his pale blue eyes. He leaned forward. "Why, this is one of the greatest stories I ever did! It's marvelous. It's got everything! Drama, character, color—"

"The plot," said Jules.

"It's sparkling and exciting, and the love interest is so tender—"

"The plot," said Jules.

"—that I almost cried myself thinking it up. Why, it's a grand story! Flashing rapiers, tall ships, brave men—"

"I already said that in the catalogue," said Jules, hopelessly. "Now I want to hear the plot. I bet you ain't got any plot at all!"

"Mike! Here I am telling him the greatest story ever written—"

"You haven't written it yet," said Mike, without turning his head.

---

4

"He's a great kidder," said Horace to Jules. "Heh, heh."

"The plot," said Jules.

"Why, sure. I was just going to tell you. It's about pirates. Not pirates, you understand, but buccaneers. Back in the days when England and France were fighting for a toehold on the Caribbean and the dons had it all sewed up. Back about sixteen hundred, just after the time of Drake—"

"We got all that in the catalogue," said Jules. "The plot!"

"Well, it's about a fellow called Tom Bristol," said Horace, thinking so hard that he squinted. "Yes, sir, it's about a fellow named Tom Bristol. A go-to-hell, swashbuckling, cut-'em-down, brawny guy who's the younger son of a noble family in England. He's a gentleman, see? But when he gets into the King's navy he don't like the admiral, and when he's given command of a ship he fights the battle his own way, and that makes the admiral mad, and so they cashier Tom Bristol from the service, even though he won the fight for them. He's too smart for them, see? And he's too hotheaded for the discipline, and so his old man, the duke, boots him out and tells him never to come back."

"Like all the other pirate novels you've written," sighed Jules.

"Like—Say, don't you think I've got artistic temperament? Do you think I've got just one story? Why, the sales on my last book—"

"Don't try to get out of this by getting mad," said Jules. "The plot! His old man, the duke, kicks him out—so what?"

"Why, so he comes to the New World. Out to St. Kitts. And there he runs into this girl. Her old man is the merchant prince of the English. He's got stacks of money that he's made by trafficking with the buccaneers, and he's really kingpin in the West Indies. And because society in St. Kitts is very swell, why, his daughter is there with him."

"With blond hair and blue eyes and very sweet—" said Jules, hopelessly.

"No!" said Horace, thinking faster. "Hell, no! She's a wild cat, see? She's turned down half the lords in England because she's looking for somebody that's really a man. She can ride to hounds and shoot better'n a musketeer, and she's a gambling fool. And she figures all these noblemen are just soft-bellied bums. No, sir, she'll never give her hand to any guy that can't beat her at any game she tackles, and she's never met such a guy. So—"

"Well, that's different enough for a heroine," said Jules. "But you know what they always say. It takes a good villain to make a story. And if you go making the villain like you did in 'Song of Arabia,' people are going to say you're slipping. Now a good villain—"

"That's what I'm getting to," said Horace, pretending to be much offended. "But you wanted the plot, and I'm giving you the plot. Now, listen. This guy Tom Bristol and the girl get together, and they like each other, but it looks like this business in the West Indies is going to fold up for England and the girl's old man because Spain is getting mighty tired of it, and so the dons figure out it's about time to wipe out all the buccaneers. So in comes this villain business. Now listen. I got it. This villain is the lord high admiral of the Spanish navy in the Caribbean, see? And this Tom Bristol mixes it up with him.

"Well, the girl's old man doesn't like Bristol because Bristol isn't rich and he hasn't got a title, and so the old man thinks he'll polish off Bristol by telling him that if he knocks hell out of the dons—why, he can have the girl. And so Bristol is fitted out with a ship to knock off a couple of Spanish ships, and with a crew of buccaneers he goes slamming off to meet this admiral—"

"That's thin," said Jules. "You gotta have a good villain. You gotta have conflict."

"Well, haven't I got it?" howled Horace.

"You ain't got any villain," said Jules.

"Now look," said Horace, "I'm telling you all about it. I'm getting to this villain. He's the lord high admiral of his Catholic majesty's navy in the Caribbean. And he gets it in 'for Bristol, too, and so they proceed to knock hell out of each other all through the book. But, of course in the end, Bristol kills the Spanish admiral and gets the girl."

"Spanish admiral, sure," said Jules. "But what kind of guy is he?"

Horace was stuck for only an instant. There was Mike, sitting at the piano, playing dolorously. There was no gauging what Mike de Wolf's ancestry really was, but it was certain that the Irish side of his family had been enjoined by one of the dons who, defeated in the Armada, were flung up on the coast of Erin to give the Irish race occasional black hair and dark eyes. Whence came the strain which made Mike what he was, he certainly could not be told from a don. Horace had his inspiration.

"Why, there's your villain," said Horace. "Now what more can you ask than that, see? Mike! Now look, Jules. Look how narrow and aristocratic his face is. Why, his nostrils are so thin that you could see light through them. And his complexion is as pale as alabaster. He's beautiful, see? He's tall and graceful, and he's got manners that'd put a king to shame. And he's got a well of sadness in him which, combined with his beauty, makes the girls fall for him in regiments. He looks delicate, but by heaven, I've seen him lick guys twice his size and weight. There's your Spanish admiral. A romantic! A poetry-reading, glamorous, hell-fighting, rapier-twisting, bowing beauty of a gentleman, all perfume and lace and wildcat. There's your Spanish admiral. And he falls in love with this girl when he gets shipwrecked on the island where she lives and she doesn't know he's a don because he's so educated he can speak English without an accent—"

Mike had begun to glare.

"You leave me out of this."

"See the fire flash in that dark eye?" said Horace to Jules. "Can't you see what he'd think of a swashbuckling captain from barbaric England? And when he gazes upon this girl who has saved his life he loses his heart to her. And not only does it become a battle between them for empire, but a conflict for a woman."

"Well—" said Jules, doubtfully, "it *sounds* pretty good. But the color—"

"The color will be perfect!" said Horace. "I know the Caribbean like I know the keys of my mill. Can't you see it now?" And he really was taking fire about the idea. "This Mike, as the Spanish admiral, will wow 'em. He's the perfect character!"

"I said to leave me out of it," said Mike. "I've got to audition in the morning, and I don't feel any too good as it is."

"Nonsense," said Horace, and faced Jules. Horace girdled the bathrobe about him and began to pace up and down the floor amid the scattered rugs from Colombia. "So there's the novel. It begins with this Bristol getting the boot like I said and then, when he's en route to the Indies, we cut the scene and we find ourselves on St. Kitts. No. We find ourselves on the deck of the *Natividad*, flagship of the Spanish fleet. This Mike is on deck, and the captain is telling him that the rest of the fleet's been scattered by the gale, and that the island off there is St. Kitts. Well, just as they're looking at the island, Mike's telescope picks out a couple of pinnaces coming out from the land. They've got a lot of men in them, and as the sea is calm and as the wind after the storm has died, why, there's no getting away from them. So this Mike says to the captain—and boy, have we got a story here!—he says, 'Pirates! Clear for action!' And so they begin to clear for action. Mike—"

Mike was trying not to listen. At the beginning of this he hadn't been feeling any too well, and now that Horace kept talking about him being on the deck of a ship and all that— Damn him, what was the idea of sticking his best friend into a story, anyway! There were a lot of things about Horace that Mike didn't quite like, such as drinking a cup of coffee halfway and then dropping cigarette butts into the cold remains, and wearing a bathrobe which hadn't been washed since Horace found it five years ago. And Horace, when he took off on a plot, was far too much to bear.

The story went on, but Mike closed his ears. He felt a little faint. An audition in the morning and if he made it then he'd be playing piano for the Philharmonic. No wonder he felt that way. But he wouldn't drink. Maybe Horace had an aspirin in the bathroom.

Unnoticed by the other two, Mike got up and tottered towards the bathroom, tagged by Horace's ringing tones. It was quite unusual for Mike to have anything go wrong with him, for his reputation, for all of his apparent pale visage, was that he could be killed only with an ax. This worried him. And the condition was such that he soon found himself barely able to navigate.

Foggily, he fumbled for the aspirin in the medicine chest, and failing to find it, reached for the light. The metal string eluded him and he sought to support himself by leaning against the washbowl.

He made contact. A blinding one! The light short-circuited with a fanfare of crackling!

Paralyzed and unable to let go, Mike sagged. He could still hear Horace as though Horace's plot was coming from Mars. He began to shiver and slump and then very quietly, he fell forward against the tub. A few seconds of consciousness remained to him and he dimly sought to pull himself up. He reached out with his hand towards the edge of the tub and then came a surge of terror which momentarily gave him animation.

Even as he reached out with that hand it was disappearing!

From fingertips to wrist to elbow!

Vanishing!

With a quiver, he shifted his fading gaze to his other hand, but it, too, was missing. And his legs were missing and his shoulders were missing—

There wasn't anything left of him at all!

The room was wheeling and dipping. He sought to howl for help. But he didn't have any mouth with which to howl.

Michael de Wolf was *gone!*

Some time after, Jules, much pleased about the plot now, got up to take his leave.

"That ought to make a fine story, Horace. When do you think you'll have it finished?"

"Oh, maybe six weeks," said Horace. "Maybe a little longer."

"Good," and then Jules looked around to say good night to Mike. But Mike was not to be seen. He never wore a hat and so there was no way to tell whether he remained in the apartment or not.

"He beat it, I guess," said Horace. "He's probably sore about my using him as a character in this story."

"He's a good one, though," smiled Jules. "Well, good night, Horace. I'll call from time to time to see how you are getting along."

"And I'll be getting right along, too," said Horace. "In fact, I'm going to start in on the first chapter right away."

Jules left and Horace pulled his machine to the forward part of the desk, brushing the alimony duns into the wastebasket. Soon there was no sound in the apartment beyond the rapid clatter of typewriter keys.

# CHAPTER
# TWO

There was roaring in his head and bitter water in his mouth, and all around him white froth and green depths intermingled furiously. Something crashed into his side, and he felt himself lifted up and cast down into silence, immediately afterwards to be torn in all directions by a savage, snarling cyclone of spray and undertow. Again he was slammed brutally into fanged rocks and heaved up and over, to land upon soggy solidity.

The next wave mauled him and tried to get him back, but he still had enough wit about him to dig his fingers into the sand and essay a crawl to a higher level. After that the surf, booming about its losses, only reached his feet.

Mike de Wolf was ill. He had swallowed a gallon or two of the sea and his stomach disliked the idea. There was blood on his hand and upon his cheek and his head ached until he had no memory whatever of what had happened to him. Exhausted, he could not move another inch up the strand. Far off sounded a rattle of musketry, but it fell upon disinterested ears. The world could have ended at that moment and Mike de Wolf would not have cared.

How long he lay there he had no way of knowing, but when he came around, the back of his neck felt scorched and he himself was hot and gritty and bothered by the flies which hovered above and settled upon his wounded head. There was no further sound of firing. Instead, there was a faint whir, reminiscent of a typewriter, which seemed to come out of the sky.

He groggily sat up. Something within was telling him that if he stayed there he would invite even further disaster. But—where else could he go?

Immediately before him were a toothy series of rocks awash in a restless sea. To his right, a craggy point reached up and out, a brownish silhouette against a crystal blue sky. Reaching away illimitably was the sea, quiet and sparkling and full of the whole spectrum.

Where was he, and why?

He turned his head and winced at the pain it brought him. Behind him lay a tangle of brown and green foliage, a wall reared up out of the gleaming yellow of the sand. This beach was not deep, and it ended at one end with the point and at the other with a tumble of gray blue stones.

He tried to rise and abandoned the effort as impossible, at least for a while.

What place was this?

A few pieces of wood were being nagged by the grasping waves. They were round and broken, and lines trailed from them. And now that he had seen them he also saw more wreckage adrift upon the waves.

Suddenly he was beset by an incredible memory. He had been standing on the deck of a galleon when two pinnaces had surged up under oars to begin to hull the tall vessel 'twixt wind and water and to sweep the decks with musketry so diabolical in its accuracy that four helmsmen in a lump were beside the wheel. And then he remembered spars coming down in a deadly rain and a musketeer in the tops diving for the sea and striking the deck instead. And the scupper ports had opened their leather mouths, and from the sodden slain a series of red rivulets gathered into one and drooled into the sea. The galleon's list had increased, and then, alone upon the quarterdeck, Mike had seen half-naked men, burned black with sun and powder, come swarming aboard, smoke sweeping back from their linstocks—

He was crazy—that was it. He'd eaten too much lobster and had had a nightmare, and it had driven him crazy. How else could one account for it?

He recollected dimly that a man in a plumed hat had bowed to him with the words: "Your lordship commands that we open fire?"

And that had been the start of the chaos.

Mike held his head in his hands, for the world was beginning to wheel and dip once more. His feeble attempt to understand his condition and his weird displacement had been too much for his sun-scorched brow.

"Your lordship?" Now why in the devil had anybody said that to him?

The sun—that was what was making him feel this way. He had to get out of it, no matter what the struggle cost him.

He was reaching forward with his right hand to take another step when the sand fountained almost between his fingers. He snatched back. A report came to him, and then several more. He stared at the rocks at one end of the beach and saw smoke spouting thickly.

Somebody was shooting at him! And he wasn't even armed!

The pain in his head vanished and he scuttled with all speed for the green-and-brown cover. When he reached it, a bullet-plucked twig smote him stingingly upon the cheek.

There was a yell and the thudding of approaching feet.

"There he went!"

"In there!"

"Get through and cut him off, the swine!"

A pistol slug plowed earth beside his foot and he crawled faster. Who the devil were these people, and why?

"Get behind him!" roared someone.

"Aye, aye, Dirk!" came from within the woods.

The sound of a horse came from the other direction on the beach. Men were threshing through the tangle and shouting to one another, coming nearer and nearer.

He felt like a rabbit, having no arms whatever. If only he had a gun or—

*Clank!*

He felt himself smitten about the waist—and lo! he had a buckler and sword! The rapier lay naked in the sling, without a scabbard, the way bravoes wore them of old. The hilt of the weapon was gold, and studded with round-cut precious stones. And in clear letters on the steel was stamped "Toledo," and "Almirante de Lobo."

Mike stood it as long as he could. The inanity of the business made him angry and the thought of lying there like a badger to be torn up by hounds gave him strength enough to rear up and grasp the hilt of the long blade and haul it free from the buckler. He took several stiff-legged strides and came out upon the sand.

Four dark-visaged swashbucklers, weapons alert, confronted him.

"There you are!" cried a black-bearded giant. "Hallo-o-o, Red, we've got the don!"

The point of the rapier licked the air.

"You'll never take me alive," said Mike. "Use your pistols, you English dogs, or I'll spit you like a roasting chicken and feed you to the sharks!"

"By gad, he's got spunk!" said Dirk, the giant, merrily. "I'll take you on meself, me bucko, and send your ears back to 'is most Catholic majesty with the compliments of me bully boys. Lay on, me lace-petticoated papist, and 'ave a taste o' Manchester steel." Dirk's cutlass flashed before Mike's calm face, and the others, drawing, rushed forward.

Assailed from four sides and, presently, from eight, Mike sent the rapier singing into the throat of one and then into the heart of another before the weapon was struck from his hand. Bare-breasted to their steel, he stood erect to receive it. And the six, with a yell, dashed in.

"*Stay!*" came a clarion voice. "Back, you gutter sweepings!" And Mike was stunned to see a great bay horse come thundering into their midst to send them sprawling, but to miss him miraculously. And he was more than stunned to see its rider.

A flame-headed woman, imperious and as lovely as any

statue from Greece, was upon the bay's side saddle. Her white linen gown was sewn with pearls about the throat and a wide hat dangled from its silken strap at her back.

"Back, I say!" she commanded. "You, Dirk! Have up the gentleman's sword and give it to him by the blade—if he'll permit a fatherless varlet to touch it!"

Mike accepted the hilt of the weapon and slid it back into the buckler.

"Begone, you wretches!" cried the girl. "Or I'll ha' ye flogged from St. Kitts!"

"Your father—" hesitated Dirk.

"Handle yer bloody business, you fumbling oaf, and I'll handle my father! Get ye hence afore my groom puts spirit into ye wi' the cat!"

They fell back away from Mike, and a Nubian nearly seven feet tall, coming up with chest heaving and skin agleam, flourished a nine-tailed lash until it screamed avidly.

Dirk and his men retreated in good order, looking back as they went, sour about the loss of a don. Fifty paces away, Dirk drew himself up and cried, "He's a Spaniard, your ladyship, and ye'll ha' a sorry time keeping him against the town!"

"You'll have a sorry time swinging from a gibbet!" cried her ladyship. "Get hence!"

The sailors went straggling out of sight beyond the boulders at the far end of the beach.

*Swish!*

*Swirl!*

Mike was cloaked in black silk! And upon his head was a wide-brimmed hat with an enormous plume!

Mike felt weak and shaky, but he swept the miraculous hat from his bare head and bowed deeply to her. Midway in this operation the world's light went on and he pitched forward on his face into the sand, his fall cushioned by the corpse of a sailor he had slain.

# CHAPTER THREE

M ike luxuriated in the huge bed. The four posts were tall sentinels guarding his rest, and if they were not enough, the doors to the place were massive enough to stop a battering ram. It was comparatively cool even here inside the netting. His head was bandaged, and his side was taped, and he smelled of rose water. He was only half awake and so his surroundings did not particularly startle him, for Mike had slept in many a bed in many a clime.

After a while he'd get up and practice and then maybe call Kurt von Rachen and have a round of golf. Summer seemed to be here in earnest. Almost tropical, it was.

A set of hinges creaked and a round black head was thrust through the door. Then more bravely the servant, clad only in a white gown, came shuffling to the bedside to lift the netting and slide the tray onto the silken coverlet. He patted up the pillows behind Mike's head and helped him sit erect and then placed the tray on his lap. As quietly, the servant went away.

Mike was coming around now. He tried to remember what friend he had who owned a place like this and had black servants. But evidently—

The memory of the encounter on the beach brought him upright so hard that he almost spilled the tray. He looked at the netting and then at the coverlet and then at the massive stone room. Somewhere a surf was beating, and nearer palms were clattering languid fronds.

Where the hell—?

He caught the tray just in time to keep from losing it. There was a fragrant melon, cool and luscious, a bottle of Madeira, a few sweet buns and a small pot of coffee. And propped against the coffee was an envelope.

Mike picked it up and read:

To the gallant captain.

"Huh," said Mike. He smelled it and found that it was old English lavender. "Hm-m-m!" said Mike.

He broke it open and found a copperplate hand had written:

SIR:

I am grieved at the discourtesy which greeted ye upon our land and beg to tender my sympathy and the hope that your woundes paine you not this day. It is not the waye of the English to morder theyre captives particularly when they have beene gallant and strong in conflicte. Please accept our guarantye of our protection and hospitalitey as a smalle payment for the injustices and horrores through which ye have been brought low. If I may so humbly request, should youre fever not be too great, I plead to attend you in your chamber come the afternoon.

LADY MARION

Mike smelled the letter again and then laid it carefully beside his pillow. He poured himself a stiff jolt of wine and downed it.

He had been in many a strange situation in his life. As a matter of fact, his life had been full of strange situations, for he had long pursued a course of dabbling with anything which happened to attract his eye, and then, when he had failed in it, to go on to something else. Music had been the only stable commodity in his restless existence, and—

Gosh! That audition!

He'd worked hard for months to get it and he'd practiced his fingers to stumps to prepare for it, and now—He made a sudden effort to get up, but it made his head throb and he sank back. Might as well have some more wine, he mused. And he did.

Where was he, and why was he? And had it been he who had lain two sailors low with a rapier?

Again he was jolted. In his realm, men who killed people usually wound up with a rope about the neck!

And, as if in answer to his misgivings, there came the sound of voices from the yard below, voices which swelled into a wave of anger. Mike listened tensely. He could not tell what the words were, but he could make out a single voice which seemed to be trying to placate the mob. Shortly, amid jeering and catcalls, the babble melted away, leaving only the surf and the palm fronds.

The black head was poked in the door again and the servant soft-footed up for the tray.

"What was all that racket?" said Mike.

"Them people from de town," said the Negro.

"What did they want?"

"Dey say mahstah more better give up Spaniard, suh. Dey say dey like hang Spaniard."

"Spaniard?"

"Yas, suh," drawled the Negro. "Dat's you, suh."

Mike blinked. "B-but why do they want to hang me?"

"Ah guess it's on account of you is a Spaniard, suh."

"Spaniard! I'm no Spaniard!"

The servant's eyes went very wide. "You isn't, suh?"

"Hell, no! I'm . . . I'm an Irishman!"

With effort, the servant brought himself back to the instructions he had received. "Missy Lady say she want know answer, suh."

"Tell her I'll see her right away," said Mike.

Lady Marion! If that had been Lady Marion on that bay, haughty and commanding and beautiful to the point of pain, Mike felt that his luck was definitely in. What a woman!

Immediately, Mike being Mike, he cast about to find some way of making himself a little more presentable. He smoothed at his hair and was startled to discover the bandage and to find how his head was throbbing under it. And when he moved, his side throbbed, too. He'd been bandaged up, it seemed, but just how he could not exactly recall. He knew that the ache in his skull was probably the reason he could not think straight. He felt he ought to be much more alarmed than he was.

Well! If Lady Marion was going to pay a call, he certainly did not want to be found in bed, undressed. At a cost of many winces, he got up the netting and put his feet on the floor. What a strangely furnished room this was! Massive chests all studded with golden nails, tapestries covering the stone walls, a shield and a battle-ax decorating the space between the windows.

Mike gave his attention to the problem of clothes. There on the chair was a pile of garments, evidently smoothed out and intended for his accouterment. Mike hobbled to them and picked them up, examining them with definite dismay. Silk stockings, black and sheer, puff-sided knee breeches, also black, and a shirt to match. And lace! There was enough lace on the cuffs of that shirt to wrap a damsel from head to toe. It was beautifully worked with gold points along the edges, but it didn't seem to Mike that lace was quite the thing to wear when meeting a lady. The lace collar was pointed to stand up behind the head and it also was heavy with gold. And the white doublet and the white half cape were braided and gold-buckled until they weighed pounds. What a weird outfit!

And yet, as he looked at it, it seemed familiar and even proper. Despite the fogginess of his head, he felt that there was something about this which harbingered a discovery of a new past stretching, fork-like, behind him.

He dropped the clothes and went searching for more appropriate gear, but nowhere could he find anything even slightly resembling tennis slacks or polo shirts.

The black servant came drifting in with the noise of a shadow. He expressed no surprise at seeing Mike out of bed; rather, he expressed surprise that Mike would seek to dress by himself.

"I help," said the servant. "Missy say when you send me, she come."

And he solemnly began to sort out the clothing on the chair, selecting the breeches as first.

Mike stared at them in dismay. They were silly-looking things. The cape he could understand, and even the doublet. But those breeches and that silken hose—

"Ole man sea raise ole Harry wit dese silks, suh. I try mah bes' to fixum, but dey don't fix so good."

"Was—was I wearing those yesterday?"

"Oh yas, suh. 'Deed you was, suh. We wouldn't have no Spaniard fashions in dis yere house, suh."

The boy seemed determined to put them on him and Mike was too groggy to resist. He was shaved and steamed and hauled at and tugged at until he closed his eyes with complete resignation. The pain in his side was terrible! And when this black boy girded up the hugely buckled belt about the doublet, Mike nearly yelped.

After a while the servant backed off from adjusting the gigantic gold buckles of the shoes and produced a brush to go to work on what of Mike's hair appeared below the head bandage. It seemed to Mike that there was quite a bit of that hair.

At last the black boy helped Mike to a full-length mirror. Mike had thought to find himself very strange and he was astonished to discover how very usual he looked to himself. In fact, it seemed to him that if he hadn't looked so, it would have been strange.

The mirror gave back the tall, supple image of a Spanish gentleman, aristocratically handsome head backed by the upstanding lace collar, pale but strong hands barely showing under the folds of gorgeous lace, slim and shapely legs backed by the flowing cape which dropped from one shoulder. He was Mike de Wolf, but somehow he wasn't Mike de Wolf. There was a commanding poise about him which was an intensification of his usual manner, and in his face showed a pride of being and a consciousness of station which the old Mike de Wolf would not have had at all. He was grand and handsome and dashing and, all in one, he was quite confused about it.

The black boy dropped the wide buckler over his shoulder and secured the sword in it. Mike almost failed to note that there was something unusual about that sword today. Its hilt was of unfaceted precious stones, set in beautifully wrought gold, and its scabbard was ornamented by two golden serpents, one on either side—The scabbard! Yesterday it had no scabbard, and Mike knew enough about swords and rapiers to know that each was fitted to its own. And he was certain, now that he thought of it, that he had not been wearing this cape when he had come through the surf.

Strange, but he could swear that he heard a typewriter running somewhere.

"You may now summon your mistress," said Mike and as he watched the boy to the door he wondered a little at his change of speech. How grandly formal had been those words, and how melodious his tones. Truly, wherever he was and why, there were some improvements which he could not discount.

He stood by the window, looking far out across an unfamiliar sea, one hand resting on the hilt of his sword, the other lightly touching the draperies at the height of his head. It was an easy, graceful pose.

The door opened and Mike did not immediately turn. He heard the rustle of silk and then the lady was bowing. He bowed low in return.

"I am indebted to your ladyship for my life," said Mike.

"And I, your lordship, am ashamed for the conduct of those sailors." She spread her loose skirts out as she sat in a carven chair and smiled upon him. "I trust your lordship is much recovered from the ill effects of the sea?"

"Thank you for your tender concern, milady. I am a little weak, but otherwise quite well." He made a slight motion towards the yard below. "I seem to be guilty of bringing threats upon your house."

"Lord Carstone cares nothing for that. He would not have you Spaniards think us murdering barbarians and he is gone even now to have a pinnace brought up into the cave of yon point to take you to safety—providing, of course, that your people can furnish some slight ransom to remove the stain of guilt from his lordship."

Mike was bewildered at the next words which nearly left his lips. And those words were, "Milady, I am Miguel Saint Raoul Maria Gonzales Sebastian de Mendoza y Toledo Francisco Juan Tomaso Guerrero de Brazo y Leon de Lobo." But they went no further than his mind. Instead, he heard himself say, "Milady, please disabuse yourself of this belief that I am a Spaniard. True, I come before you clothed as an accursed don and true, I was aboard the *Natividad* during the action, but I, milady, have the honor of being Michael O'Brien, an Irish gentleman of family, at your service and indebted to you for your hospitality."

She looked incredulously at him, at his Spanish cape and Toledo sword, at the pale aristocracy of his visage and the slender body within the silk.

"Not a Spaniard? God's breath, milord, you jest!"

"That I resemble a don, I avow. When the great armada of his most Catholic majesty was smashed by the brave English a few decades ago, my grandfather was cast up on the shore of Ireland, storm driven and perishing. He was taken into the castle of Lord Dunalden, and there met my grandmother, his future wife, an Irish gentlewoman. I am the last of their family and, much against my own wishes, I sought my fortune in Spain. I was being sent here to the West Indies to take command of a mine when our fortunate accident took place off this island. I care nothing for my

Spanish forebears after I have been with them. I repeat, milady, that I am an Irish gentlemen, unfortunately part Spanish, thrown upon your mercies and your hospitality. If I must pay ransom, then let it be sufficient unto the dignity of a Dunalden."

Plainly, she was fascinated by him. Her tawny eyes examined him more minutely, and her lips were a little parted with wonder at him.

"Then—then you were not in command of that Spanish vessel?"

"I was not, milady," said Mike and knew that he lied, but was powerless to correct that lie.

"You—you are a Dunalden?"

"Aye, milady. That I am also Spanish is only a whim of the Almighty."

"Prithee, milord," she said, standing, "have no fears of your treatment in this house. You are welcome as long as you like, for we must be given a chance to wipe away this ill-considered insult. Lord Carstone will be pleased at your presence tonight at supper. And now I must not further weary you. Good afternoon, milord."

Mike bowed deeply and felt his side was being torn out of him. He watched her as she went through the door, side or no side, for she had a graceful, regal way of walking which made him warm all through.

When she was gone he sank down on the bed and lay out at full length. Gee, what a woman! She was about five feet nine—some four inches shorter than Mike—and she had the poise of a queen. But she needed no crown. She had been born with it—her hair. How long and lovely she was! More of flame than of flesh. And those eyes—When they raked him they bathed him with ecstasy! Never had Mike— even Mike!—seen a woman like her.

And then, slowly, thoughts of her became confused in his own puzzle. Where was he? Why? And what time? Surely no woman had worn clothes like that since the early seventeenth century. Pearls in her hair where they made her coiffure flame the more, a great lace collar about her sweet throat to make her skin seem all the more white by contrast, a tight-bodiced gown which set off every curve of her delicious figure—She was something out of Van Dyck! All blue of gown, cream of lace, red of hair. And his thoughts drifted back slowly again to his problem.

Evidently, Mike decided, he had received a knock on the head which had brought on delusions. Yes, that must be it. And he felt sorry for himself. Besides, his head did ache dreadfully, and he loosened his collar and shed his cape in order to relax and try to sleep. Maybe when he woke all this would be gone and he would be back in time for his audition with the Philharmonic. He'd have to tell Horace about this. Might make a good yarn for him—

He sat upright so abruptly that he nearly tore his head off.

Horace!

Horace Hackett!

Why, he'd been talking about buccaneers and the West Indies and Spanish gentlemen and a hero named Tom Bristol—The light cord, the vanishing limbs—And Horace had said Mike was the perfect part for the villain of the piece—And Jules had grinned and agreed—

Horace Hackett! And his novel, "Blood and Loot," a tale of buccaneering on the Spanish Main when the English and French sought to stem the tide of the Spaniards and wrench from them some of the riches grasped in the early days of discovery.

"Blood and Loot," by Horace Hackett!

Then Mike grinned wearily. Well, that was that. He'd been listening to the plot and he'd got a knock on the head and now, of course, he was dreaming. Well, 'twas a pity to abandon such a lovely lady, but a dream was only a dream, and one had to get some more sleep to audition at the Philharmonic. Ho-hum. And Mike de Wolf, convinced as a dreamer is always convinced that he was not even awake, went off to sleep.

Some hours later Mike awoke and the room was dark. A few stars twinkled in the rectangle of open window and the surf was quiet. The palm fronds no longer rattled. Mike, yawning, reached for the table where he always kept his cigarettes but there was no table. He reached further. Still no table. Instead, his questing hand connected with a bell cord and to steady himself he gave it a strain. Somewhere near a bell jingled and the black servant slid in, carrying a taper.

Mike stared at the fellow in disbelief. He had sold himself the dream idea so completely—

"Supper ready in mos' an hour, suh," said the boy. Like a white-gowned ghost he went drifting through the room, lighting tapers. One by one the objects appeared which Mike had seen before. And then, looking down at himself, he saw that while his shoes had been removed while he slept, he was still clothed as before.

"Boy!"

"Mah name Jimbo, suh."

"Boy, what's the date?"

"Don' guess Ah knows whut you is talkin' about, suh. We ain't got no mo' eatin' dates, iffen that's whut you means."

"The date," persisted Mike. "The month, the day, the year."

"Seems like I heerd somebody say this was somethin' like sixteen hunnert and forty, suh, but Ah wouldn' know."

"What?"

Mike was so startled by the statement that the boy, Jimbo, almost dropped the taper.

"That's three hundred years ago!" wailed Mike. "That's impossible!"

He slumped back on his pillow and stared groggily at a lizard which walked upon the ceiling, stalking a fly. Sixteen hundred and forty! These clothes matched the date. So did his rapier, the ship yesterday, the sailors, the Lady Marion's speech, and her clothes—all, all added up to sixteen forty! And yet—somehow it wasn't.

He had heard of time travel and he'd also heard of lunacy and the way he felt right now, he was more willing to grant the latter. Was this a movie set made of cheesecloth and propped with sticks? That thought brought him up and made him kick the wall, but hobbling about and nursing his wounded toe, he decided that it was not a movie set and made the decision with profanity.

When Mike quieted he fell to wondering on the battle of yesterday. He remembered it very clearly now, recalled the soul-shaking thunder of cannon and the nasty sight of men being torn in half by chain shot and the all-too-real screams of suddenly shattered humanity. That battle had been no fake. And when he had run his rapier through those sailors on the beach, that had been honest-to-God blood and their death throes could not have been simulated.

Something else was coming over him now, a sort of strange belief in all this and a belief in his own part in it. Time travel? Well, if it was time travel, then how was it that he had managed the ship out there, knowing all its parts, giving the necessary orders, feeling a hatred towards the enemy which would never have existed in the heart of one who was wholly strange to the scene. No, he was not strange to this place or this time, for he had memory of it which, dim though it was, ran currently with his own life memory. And yet the memory did not seem anything from the past but from the immediate present.

Again he tried to lay aside the thought that this was "Blood and Loot," product of Horace Hackett's fertile if somewhat distorted imagination. These names, his own character, even this plot—Oh, no! My God, not that! Why, that would mean that he was Horace Hackett's villain in truth and in the flesh. And it would mean that he was in a never-never land where anything might and probably would happen. Where time would be distorted and places scrambled and distances jumbled and people single-track of character—Oh, Lord, not "Blood and Loot."

A horrible thought took him then and froze him to the bed. Horace Hackett's villains always suffered a frightful fate!

No, no, no, no, no, no, no!!!

Not "Blood and Loot!"

He was just going through a delusion brought on by that electric shock. He was just living in his own dreams after hearing Horace Hackett outline a plot. This place could not exist at all, either in time or in space.

Still—and he attempted to fend off that gruesome conclusion—he was definitely awake and sufficiently in his right mind to realize this was all wrong.

And if this was the Spanish Main in the year 1640, and if these people were English gentlefolk, and if those sailors had been Brethren of the Coast, and if he was Miguel Saint Raoul de Lobo, almirante of the fleets of his most Catholic majesty, then b'heaven and gadzooks, this was the last island in the world where he should be! His strangely entangled memories gave off some facts about what happened to captives in this undeclared war.

He'd escape, that's what he'd do. And instantly he was reminded within himself that there were Caribs on this island in the interior and that Caribs thought white flesh a luscious banquet. And besides he couldn't escape, for what did he know about these guns and sword fighting and sailing a ship? If he tried to fight free, that would be the end of him. In the interior he would be eaten. At sea he would drown. If he stayed here he'd be discovered and strung on a gibbet—

No, no, no! This wasn't Horace Hackett's "Blood and Loot!" It couldn't be! It was just a nightmare. It *had* to be!

Jimbo fixed him up again and then helped him down the stairs. Mike was pleased to find that his side hurt much less and that his head did not ache at all. And again there was that sound of a typewriter.

---

He walked through a long hall and into a room where tall candles gleamed above gold dishes and crystal and found Lady Marion there before him. He bowed elegantly to her— amazed at this graceful accomplishment of his—and she curtsied deeply back. His eyes were so taken up with her— for her gown was now amber, like her eyes, and cut very low at the front and back—that he failed to see Lord Carstone until a "Harumph! Har-r-r-umph!" appraised him of that presence.

He bowed again to Carstone.

The fellow was almost as broad as tall, an overly uphol- stered giant sculped out of lard. Great gold chains gleamed against a flowered vest and green and red-patterned coat; his calves bulged out of strained white stockings and there were artificial roses on his shoes. His wigged head was a lump of putty sunk into a huge roll of cotton. All seven chins wobbled as he spoke.

"Milord," said Mike, "I am pleased at last having the plea- sure of meeting my gracious host."

"Harumph, harumph," said Lord Carstone. "M'daughter tells me yer Irish, sir."

"I have that honor, milord."

Carstone inspected him. "Damme if ye don't look like a don. Well, well! Harumph, har-r-r-umph, my error. M'pardon, sir, and I bid ye welcome to my house. Gog's wounds, Marion, my wench, if he doesn't look like a double-damned don, at that! Well, no mind, no mind. Sit yerself down and have at it, m' boy."

Mike seated Marion at the foot of the board and took his own station in the middle. But dinner was not yet to begin, for with a clank and a creak there entered a scarlet-coated, gold-braided, white-wigged, powdered fellow of about middle age, whose bearing and address were those of a soldier.

"Hah, Capt'n!" said Carstone. "In time, I see, for dinner as usual, eh? This is Michael O'Brien, an Irish gentleman whom we mistook for a don. Sir, Capt'n Braumley."

"Pleased and honored," said Mike, getting up and bowing. The captain bowed doubtfully and took his seat with a clatter of weapons across from the guest. Captain Braumley's battle-battered face was a little antagonistic.

"So it's Irish, is it? Blast m' blood and bones, what's this?" He looked hard at Mike. "Can't say as I've any belly for sitting to dine with a Spaniard papist!"

"Ye'll keep yer evil tongue in yer cheek, sir," said Marion with lifted chin, "or I'll have ye taught better manners by the gentleman himself. He 's no common gutter-bred soldier!"

The captain choked on that one and became purple-hued. Mike had never seen anyone really turn purple from embarrassment before, and it was really amazing to see it. Bright purple.

"He's a gentleman and he's at m'board," said Carstone heavily, "and if ye can't be civil he's welcome to run you through a time or two."

The fact that they both insisted on the fact that Mike was a gentleman seemed to mollify the captain at least to the point of civility. That the captain was not a gentleman he soon proved by his address to his dinner, which was as overbearing as his presence on a parade ground and quite as loud.

"Forgive 'm," said Carstone to Mike. "You do look damned like a don. Fact, they're talkin' o' catchin' and hangin' ye in the public square and burnin' ye in the bargain, so don't be too hard on the captain."

Being a gentleman was evidently important, thought Mike. But it didn't make one immune from villagers.

"Hanging and burning?" he said, spoon poised over his soup.

"Aye. Ye killed two sailors, I hear, and a damned capable piece of work too, what's more. Throat and heart. Have you teach the capt'n here a trick or two with the sword, eh?"

The captain glowered but went on with his frontal attack, evidently supposing his beef still on the hoof.

Dinner sped by, plate by plate, and Mike was becoming groggy with the profusion of various kinds of meat when at last the parade stopped and the rear guard of wine began to come up.

"So yer Irish," said the captain.

"Aye," said Mike. "An' I take my mother's maiden name of O'Brien."

The captain thought he saw a joke in that and looked sly. "Was anythin' wrong with yer father's, or didn' ye ever know it?"

Carstone spilled his wine. Lady Marion went white and stood up so fast that the black servant behind her barely had time to get her chair out of the way.

"Sir," Mike heard himself say, "my grandfather was Martine Sebastian Jose Ignacio Tomaso Guerrero de Brazo y Leon, Knight of the Golden Fleece, Captain of the Cross, Lord of Toledo and Seville. My father, sirrah, was Lord Follingby, Terrence O'Brien."

"Then you *are* a don, b'heaven!" cried the captain. "Guts and gadflies, Carstone, ye'll have a don at your board and keep him from the town! I'll have my garrison here within an hour!"

"You'll be dead within an hour," said Mike coolly. And his blade leaped from its scabbard and flashed as it danced across the board. He leaped between the tall candles and jumped down in such a way as to bar the exit of the captain.

"I'll not kill you with this for it takes no stain of filthy blood," said Mike. "But pistols, Lord Carstone, are in order for two."

"B-but you're really a don!" said Carstone.

"I choose to call myself Irish and my allegiance is English," said Mike. "If the clod here can stomach the pistol's mouth, have them out and we'll to it!"

"You call me coward!" roared the captain, his own blade shrieking from its sheath.

Mike was forced to give way before the lightning thrusts which sought his throat. For an instant he was paralyzed by the certain knowledge that he knew nothing whatever about swordsmanship! The singing steel blades clashed with desperate thrust and more desperate parry and Mike went up the stairs of the hall two steps. He knew he needed all his eyes for that magically shifting point which sought his heart or throat and yet he amazed himself by saying coolly, "Your permission, milady. The beggar seems a bit insistent."

What the devil made him talk like this? And was that sound he heard a typewriter?

It *must* be!

Marion stood in the doorway of the dining room, light from the lantern there throwing molten beams into her hair. Her lips were parted in fascination and her eyes were overbright.

Mike went through the other's guard in a false return, leaped back, parried with a quick cutover and attacked with a flying return so swift and adroit that Captain

Braumley was disarmed so suddenly that he stood staring at his empty hand, while his rapier went clanging over the stones to bring up loudly against the wall.

Mike then used his blade as a whip and begin to cut the low-born captain about the back and buttocks until Braumley howled in pain and protest at the abuse, stumbling backwards and striving to fend off that merciless blade with his extended hands.

"I apologize!" wailed Braumley.

"Out, offal," said Mike, catapulting the fellow through the door and down the long curving steps. And when Braumley had fallen the flight, Mike seized the fellow's sword and flung it after him.

Leaning upon his sword at the top of the steps, Mike said, "Thank your pagan god, blackguard, that you're an oaf and no gentleman, else my clean blade would have drunk your blood to death!"

Braumley, moaning, picked himself out of the refuse in the yard and, retrieving his sword, slunk swiftly off into the gateway and down the hill to the town.

Mike turned with a gallant bow to the Lady Marion. "Forgive me, milady."

Her voice was throaty with emotion. "He—he insulted you in our house. The—the right was yours—"

"Then I am forgiven?" said Mike.

"Aye," she said, faint-voiced.

And then she fled down the hall and closed the door of the drawing room behind her.

Mike went back to Carstone, who poured him a glass.

"Sorry, sir," said Mike.

"Oh, bosh and fiddlesticks, m' lad; these things happen. Frightful bore, anyway. Drank m' wine and made love t' me daughter. Swine, swine clear through, m' lad. Have another glass. Cawn't say I've enjoyed anything so much since my brindle bull whipped Snarling Laddy in '21. Besides, I owed him money."

"I trust I didn't frighten Lady Marion too much."

"Frighten! *Hah*! Why, m' lad, there's a wench! There, m' lad, is a wench. Damme if she didn't run away, at that. Show, all show. You'll know these women after a time. Dare say when yer as old as I am and you've known as many, you'll understand. But there's a wench, that Marion. She thinks she's sick at the sight of blood and violence, but what are women but violence and blood, what? I say, m' lad, I'd never question the word of a gentleman, but are you sure you weren't in command of that ship out there the other day?"

"I?" said Mike, smiling.

"Well, we've had a bad time about dons. Papists and all that. Lord Buck'n'h'm—Steenie, you know—made all sorts of blather over papists. He's dead, but the English are still stirred up about the dons. Now, bein' a political power, I know somethin' about it and religion—well, what's religion? I make no bones about it, damme eyes. I want what the Spaniards have, and so I'm made to preach against 'm. Y' know, most of m' trade is done with the buccaneers, and so we keep 'em worked up about the dons. Well, have another glass. A man can't help his grandfather. Lord of Toledo and Seville, you say? Well, well. I'd say there's only one don I'd like to see swing, and that's the fellow they call Miguel Saint Raoul de Lobo, lord high admiral of his most Catholic majesty's navies in the New World."

Mike felt a jolt and a realization of identity with that same lord high admiral. In fact, it was coming to him that he *had* commanded the *Natividad* in the recent action, and *was* Miguel Saint Raoul de Lobo. He felt faint, but he heard himself say, offhand, "Yes? Can't say as I know the gentleman. What have you against him in particular?"

"Well, m' lad, I'm a businessman and a good one. England may have no right at all to these colonies, but as long as I can keep the buccaneers hard at it—the English and the French both—why, the Spanish cargoes find their way to England through my clearing house. We might as well be frank about it. It's damned good business. Spain is rich. Why should she begrudge a few millions in bullion? Eh? And these seas are swarmin' right now with English and

French adventurers. So business is very good. But m' intelligences from Spain tell me the dons are sick of it. They've sent an admiral, and a good one, out here. Not one of your pap-suckling pansies but a fellow that distinguished himself in the recent unpleasantness against th' English. But I'll ha' nothing to worry about soon."

"So?" said Mike.

"Aye. Y' see, there's a young chap name of Bristol, good family but wild, cashiered from the navy he was, that come out here to seek 'is fortune. Impressed Marion no end, and she gathered up his eyes and she's still got 'm. Likely lad, but wild. All steel and cannon shot, that's Bristol. Good-lookin' too. 'E come down here to take his ease with the Brethren of the Coast, and soon as they found out he was an ex-naval captain they gathered 'round. So, not wantin' to stop in the way of the lad, I outfitted a bit of a fleet to see how many cargoes he can bring back. I've faith in 'm, though I'd never let 'm know it. If he comes back with a good haul, why, the lads'll be tearing to go to sea at his heels again, and we've a force against Spain. If he's the boy he started out to be, why, there's even a chance that we can take a colony or two from the dons. I've given 'm letters o' mark as governor of this island, and I've offered him the hand of Marion herself if he can come back here with the head of this fancy lord high admiral dangling under his bowsprit."

"Quite a prize," said Mike, jealously.

---

"Aye, quite a prize. If I hadn't done it, Bristol might not have tackled any Spanish first-line vessels. He'll be back here in a week or two, God willing, and he's hoping to bring home the pride of the navy of Spain as aforesaid."

"Head under the bowsprit, eh?" said Mike.

"Even that. If not now, then some day. The Spanish, y'know, sent this Miguel Saint Raoul de Lobo here to wipe up the English and the coast brethren, and what a joke on his lordship to come home under a bowsprit!"

"How—how," said Mike faintly, "will he know if he has the right man?"

"Why, 'tis simple. He's got some Maroons from the Panama coast that were slaves on the flagship when his lordship came over from Spain. They know him. Y' see, if we get him, we get the one man who had orders to wipe out the English, and we'll discourage another from taking the field against our thriving little colonies. Neat, eh?"

"You mean—mean that these Maroons will betray his lordship?"

"Betray! Why, 'tis plain to see you don't know this coast, m' lad. The Spaniards murdered Maroons until their arms were tired, and Maroons are fast friends of the buccaneers. They even wanted Bristol to go to the home where his lordship first put up and take 'm in 'is sleep. And maybe they'll do it. You can't beat a proud man like a Maroon and murder his wife and friends without him doing something about it, Indian or no Indian!"

---

"I dare say," said Mike, and memories were stirring uneasily where no past had been. "And this Bristol will soon be home, eh?"

"Right."

"By the way, milord, I'd like quite well to stay, but I can't have the town revolting against you because of my father and because of this Captain Braumley."

"But yer English sympathies and the word of a gentleman protect you," said Lord Carstone, all chins wagging. "And as for Braumley and all, he's no loss. I've but to say what happened. Damme, who's governor here? And you knowing Spanish—why, you can be of great help to me. In an intelligence way, you know."

Mike received the impact of the reason why Lord Carstone was being so nice to him. Mike could be so neatly used in this business that Carstone's eagerness quite blinded him to Mike's possible duplicity. A spy to the Spanish, indeed. In the pay of the English! Unaccountably, Mike broiled within at the thought. But the fact was saving his life. For he, Miguel Saint Raoul de Lobo, lord high admiral of his most Catholic majesty's navy in the New World, would not last long the instant one Tom Bristol arrived home. His command of English, a thing so rare as nearly to excuse his "Spanish father," would not serve him once those Maroons laid eyes on him. He had a vision of raw-backed men dying in the sun while the lash still swooped down upon them, and gutted women lying in the charred wreckage of forest huts, and babies with their skulls smashed against rocks—Maroons! How they hated the Spanish. And with what cause!

He tried valiantly to figure an avoidance of the necessity to stay here until Bristol arrived. But a panting black brought news which saved his energy.

"Mah lord," said the black, bowing to the floor, "guard say come run and tell quick. Cap'n Bristol just now pass he fleet in by light."

And the thunder of saluting guns tore apart the night to confirm the news.

# CHAPTER FOUR

In the cool, dark depths of the Vagabond Club on Fifty-fourth Street, Horace Hackett limply regarded a half-empty glass, a perfect picture of an author who has finished a day's stint and who hopes his virtuousness will be noticed. His sports coat was unbuttoned to relax his rotundity and his pink-and-purple tie was askew; he needed a shave and seemed to be in a bad state of disrepair, hair in eyes and cuffs none too clean.

He was wholly unconscious—so far as anyone could tell—of the whisper across the room, to wit: "That's Horace Hackett, the popular novelist." And it was purely coincidental that Horace immediately sighed deeply and assumed a profound expression.

Winchester Remington Colt, the western writer, came lounging into the bar, his Stetson on the back of his head, his high-heeled boots loud upon the mosaic.

"Gimme a shot of redeye, pard," he said to the English bartender.

And because the English bartender was used to the various artists and writers and publishers who belonged to the Vagabond Club, he knew already that this meant a drink of King's Colony Scotch in soda, weak.

Winchester Remington Colt wrapped a pale hand around the glass and came striding along, having spotted Horace.

"Hello, Hackett, ole pard," said Colt. "Mind if I hunker down a spell? Reckon as how you been horsewhippin' the wordage from the way yore all tuckered out." He was wholly oblivious of the whisper from the end of the room:

"That's Winchester Remington Colt, the western writer."

"Worn to the bone," sighed Horace, extending a hand so that Colt could see how his fingers were shaking. They weren't, and so Horace made them shake a little. Colt wondered if Horace had ever bothered to clean his fingernails in his life.

"Book, I suppose," said Colt. "Doing a book myself. It's about—"

"Yes," said Horace hurriedly, "a book. Deadline right up on me, practically feeding it to the presses. It's called 'Blood and Loot,' a story of—"

"Is that so?" said Colt, his western jargon getting lost now that he was talking in lowered tones to Horace. "My story is right up against the press, too. It's a fine yarn, though. Splendid setting. Early Southwest. Unusual, too. This sheriff has a son who isn't any good and so when everybody accuses the boy of holding up the Wells Fargo office at—"

"Sounds fine," said Horace. "Yes, sounds fine. This 'Blood and Loot' is a story of the early buccaneers. You know, lace and tall ships and rapiers and two men fighting to the death over a lovely woman—"

"Is that so?" said Winchester Remington Colt, swiftly. "'Hell on the Border' has a swell heroine. She's a dance-hall girl that's trying to go straight, see? And so when she falls in love with the sheriff's son—"

"Well, well, well!" said Horace. "That does sound fine."

They gave up and sat moodily sipping their drinks. At last the plot-recital contest which so often baffles authors died out within them and they began to chat generally.

"This is a hell of a business," said Horace. "If I had it all to do over again, I would dig ditches for a living."

"So would I," said Colt. "Work, work, work, and where's it get you. Some day you turn in a sour one and then they say, 'Colt's slipping. He's a has-been.' And they forget about all the money you've made for them and they shake their heads. And then they're convinced that you're through and so everything you send in gets put into the slush pile and read by the fourth assistant editor, and after a while they don't even send letters, just printed rejection slips. It's a hell of a life."

"Yeah," said Horace. "Just as if everybody didn't lay an egg at one time or another. It'd be different if editors were different."

"They're all a pack of bums," said Colt. "And what makes it so awful is that they never really know what the public wants. Why, sometimes you get a story through that they think stinks and the public eats it up. And sometimes the story really does stink and the public eats it up just the same."

"Yeah," said Horace. "Remember 'Gone With the Wind'?"

"Huh?"

" 'Gone With the Wind.' All the waitresses and bus drivers thought it was swell and what'd it have on the ball? Nothing, that's what. Any professional writer could really have done a good job on it."

"Oh, sure. I remember now. It was about a young guy whose father was out to kill him."

"Yeah," said Horace.

"Or was that 'Anthony Adverse'?"

"Yeah," said Horace. "But the point is, editors make me

sick. They burn you out and squeeze you dry, and then they say you're a has-been. I ought to buy a farm."

"Farm?" said Winchester Remington Colt, stretching out his high-heeled boots. "I was on a farm once. For a weekend. Hell of a place. Woke me up at ten o'clock in the morning they did, after me not being able to sleep all night because it was so quiet."

They felt perfectly in accord now.

After a little, Horace said: "You know, I've been running across a funny thing lately."

"Yeah?" said Colt.

"I find out that it's a lot of bunk plotting the middle of stories out straight."

"How so?"

"Well, you get them going and they pretty near write themselves. That is, if the characters are good."

"Yeah. I've noticed that once in a while. You start a story and then it takes itself out of your hands and begins to go off as it pleases. Yeah, I've noticed that."

"Sure. You lay out the beginning and know how it's going to end, and it wanders around as it pleases in the middle. 'Course, you know the high spots, but even those take care of themselves pretty well if you have the effect you want in mind. This one I'm doing now started out to be a straight proposition, with the hero coming in as usual and getting mopped up by the villain and then mopping up the villain. But after I got it going I found out that the villain was a pretty interesting character, too, and so the thing is going to be pretty hot. Sympathetic from both sides, see? I figure, maybe, a villain as a straight villain is pretty hard to swallow. You know, a guy isn't all bad. So the villain's got his reasons, too. Now in this story the villain is going to fall in love with the heroine and it's going to make him as decent as can be. 'Course, he pulls a couple of dirty tricks and gives the hero some thinking, and there's a lot of fighting around, but the thing is handling itself, if you get what I mean."

"Sure, that happened to me in 'Hell on the Rio Grande.' It just rattled itself off as though I didn't have a thing to do with it. Sure I knew the beginning and the end, but the middle just went racing along."

"It's funny," said Horace. "I get spooky about it sometimes. It's—well, it's as if we were perfectly in tune with the story. We don't have to think about it, it just sort of comes bubbling out of us like music."

"Yeah. I remember Mike saying one time that a story wasn't any good unless it came out that way. But then, he's nutty on the subject of music and so it doesn't count. By the way, haven't seen him. He was supposed to come over to my apartment for a cocktail party last night, and he didn't show up. You seen him?"

"No. I think he got mad at me for saying I was going to use him for a story. He shoved off and I haven't seen him since. But what I was getting at is the way you feel about stories sometimes. It's—well, sort of divine, somehow. Here we are able to make and break characters and tangle up their lives and all, and sometimes the characters get so big for us that they sort of write themselves, if you know what I mean."

"And you get a real kick out of writing it," said Colt. "You know how it's going to end, but you surprise yourself in the middle. Sure."

"Sure. Now I know how I started it and I know the conflicts and I know that in the end the hero knocks the villain off and gets the girl, but just how it's all going to happen I'm not sure. It just sort of happens."

"Yeah. Makes a guy feel funny. Like he's a medium, or something."

"No, I feel different than that. When I go knocking out the wordage and really get interested in my characters it almost makes me feel like—a god or something."

"Yeah, I know," said Colt.

"It's a great business," said Horace.

"Yeah. Sure. Nothing like being a writer."

---

# CHAPTER
# FIVE

Mike de Wolf wandered in perplexity through the governor's great stone house. A year or two before this displacement into an apparent nowhere, he had cruised the West Indies briefly in an attempt to shake off a siege of melancholy boredom. He had painted a few pictures of red-roofed houses and native women with baskets on their heads and had then tossed the canvases overboard on the decision that he would never be able to paint—and he had seen St. Kitts from the windows of an automobile hired by tourist companions who had bored him desperately.

Now, going to the great windows of a drawing room, looking down the hill from over the battlements to the town, he was recalled to an earlier visit here. This was Brimstone Hill, then. But how strange to find this mighty fortress all built and wholly solid if the year was 1640! This great fortress, he remembered out of the tourist's guide, was built after the American Revolution! And yet he had twice checked the date, and it was agreed that the year was 1640. In addition, as well as he could remember, there was something wrong with the geography. The harbor was nearly circular and admission to it was gained through a very proper channel all set with flashing lights. He wasn't sure, but he supposed flashing lights to be a fairly modern invention.

Where was he, and why?

Brimstone Hill in St. Kitts solved it not at all, for this was not really Brimstone Hill and it was not really St. Kitts. And the dates were shuffled like the numbers on a deck of cards.

Late eighteenth-century masonry in the mid-seventeenth century.

A twentieth-century dilettante of the arts masquerading as a Spanish admiral in 1640.

And if this was St. Kitts, then where were the French, with whom the government had been shared by the British? And where was Sir Thomas Warner, who history said had been governor and practical owner of the place at this stated period?

Certainly this sort of thing would soon drive him mad. Nothing could be trusted. The first thing he knew, somebody would pull out a cigarette lighter and reach for a telephone, the while speaking archaic English on the subject of the doings of Charles I.

He moved out upon the balcony the better to see activity in the harbor. He felt assured that if he tried to escape from this place he would be stopped and suspected, and yet— Gog's blood, as Lord Carstone would say, he didn't dare stay here and face Captain Bristol and the Maroons! There were the vessels, all lights and activity, anchor chains rattling out as they took their anchorages. Seven there were, most of them small, about two hundred tons. Their type was difficult to establish for lack of daylight.

Where was he, and why?

He hadn't moved back into history, for history had never been thus, and so any time change was out. He hadn't ascended to another plane, for too much of this was definitely human earth.

His first guess about Horace Hackett had sent a chill prickling at the hairs of his neck. The last thing he had heard had been exactly this plot. "Blood and Loot" had contained these names . . . He revolted against the idea. Not Horace Hackett's story!

He had an image of Horace, girded about with a dirty bathrobe, surrounded by cigarette butts, unshaven and sweaty, hammering thunderously upon his typewriter, ripping off copy by the yard.

Mike cast his mind back over the events of the past two days. Two men he had killed on the beach and wounded another tonight. And he had bested them with a rapier—a weapon about which he knew nothing, but which in his hands became abrupt demise. And there was something else—his head felt quite all right and the bandage about it had mysteriously vanished; further, his side felt as good as new and there was no pull of tape there. What mad world was this in which a man became possessed of sudden talents and healed in minutes? And then his sword scabbard and cape and hat had appeared magically overnight.

His own conduct and his speech had not been Mike de Wolf. Could it be that he was actually taking on the character of one Miguel Saint Raoul de Lobo, lord high admiral of the Spanish fleet in the Caribbean? Certainly his memory was becoming padded with odd memories which had no identity with his own (Mike's) past.

He was recalling just now that a woman named Anne awaited at Nombre de Dios to call him "dear," and that a Carib slave girl, a princess among her savagely beautiful people, sat watching the sea from the window of a balconied casa. He was remembering the thin, rapacious evil called Father Mercy and the giant Trombo, so ready with a cat or a headsman's ax and so devoted to his admiral.

He was remembering a yesterday of play amid orange blossoms at Valencia and a proud Spanish mother and father looking fondly upon him as a cadet of the king; a kiss stolen in Morocco; the thunder of his vessels' guns at Gonai; the shrieks of men dying in a mist of smoke; the whimper of wounded in the dark; the soft hands of a pope making him a Knight of the Cross; soft, sweet arms in the hot humidity of Panama; the dance of a buccaneer swinging from a gibbet; dispatches from the king . . .

His hands whipped to his doublet and parchment crackled there. He took out the packets with their broken seals, sea-stained and wrinkled, but proud with the arms of Castile and Leon. By the light of a guttering guard lantern he glanced at them.

How familiar was that language! Spanish, but as clear as any English!

## ALMIRANTE:

The English and French bore like evil worms into the glorious Empire of Spain beyond the seas, sacking cities and flaunting our troops and governors. You are given, as enclosed, commissions as lord high admiral of his most Catholic majesty's navies in the New World, empowered to use all vessels and forces of defense and offense to put down forever the English and French dogs. You are to take no cognizance of any letters or commissions but are to hang buccaneers as pirates wherever found. You are to wipe out the coastal villages of any Caribbean Indians found to be aiding the English and French. This is not official war and your discretion is solicited while your utmost endeavor is requested. May you again arise victorious above our enemies upon the sea and keep glorious the golden banner of your native land.

PHILIPPE
KING

Mike had the idea that he had read these before, but their import now was staggering. Dispatches such as these upon his person! And Braumley barking at the landing that a Spaniard was in the house of the governor. And from what he had heard of this Captain Bristol, he doubted not that the man would be thorough and demand that his Maroons be allowed to see the Spaniard. And these dispatches— they would mean his death! But he dared not destroy them and thus destroy his own authority. He swiftly replaced the papers in his doublet, glancing about to see that no one had seen.

He was barely in time, for a soft footfall sounded near him on the parapet.

It was Lady Marion.

She had not seen him yet, for she was studying the harbor below, and Mike felt a sudden jealous pang.

"Milady," he said.

She started and then smiled uncertainly at him.

"The unfortunate lesson merited by Captain Braumley and administered by myself seems to have upset you. Forgive such actions on my part. . . ."

Good Lord! What was wrong with him that he had to talk in such a stilted way? And—*Yes*! There was the sound of that typewriter again!

"They are already forgiven, sir."

"Again, I thank you." And he bowed.

They stood there for a little time, looking down the steep hill at the fleet in the harbor, yellow jewels set sparkling into black satin. Mike looked at Lady Marion as much as he could without staring. She had drawn a thin white wrap about her shoulders against the cool wind and the high collar of it put an outer halo about the halo of her hair. Mike thought about paintings of the masters and could find no face to compare with hers, no coloring to match the vibrant life of her own.

"Soon you will meet Captain Bristol," said Lady Marion at last. "I hope you will like him."

"My affections," said Mike, "are yours to command."

"He might—hold your Spanish grandfather against you. I hope you will understand that he was once confined in a Spanish prison when a storm drove him onto the reefs of Spain, and was tried by the Inquisition and condemned to the auto-da-fé as an English heretic. With great skill and courage he managed his escape, but had to leave many of his crew to die or wear out their lives on the galleys. He is bitter."

"Is that why he seeks the Spaniard in these waters?"

"Aye, and other things. We have a right to this sea, and Captain Bristol believes it can be enforced."

"He is most optimistic, judging from what I have seen of the fleets of Spain."

"His men are wild devils," said Lady Marion. "The deadliest marksmen in the world are the buccaneers who made their living shooting cattle and other wild game in Hispaniola. They are the restless spirits who chafed under navy discipline and managed to desert, who flouted authority and order and came out to the New World in prison ships or merchantmen. Only Captain Bristol has been able to unite them into a fleet and there is much hope that the power of Spain may be broken in these colonies."

"So Bristol dreams of the wealth of Peru," said Mike.

"Aye. And the power of the 'bloody flag,'" replied Lady Marion. "Some day the cross of St. George and not the cross of Spain will float above the Caribbean."

"You seem to share the ambitions of your men," said Mike.

"Of Lord Carstone, sir."

"From the way he talked about you this evening, he seems quite well pleased with the daughter he has raised. And with reason."

She looked musingly down across the harbor and then, withdrawing from the battlement, wandered into the castle hall, Mike keeping beside her.

"There was a time, sir, when my father was not pleased," she said. "For a girl in the family of a great merchant is no asset—and he never had a son."

"But that is all forgotten. It must be, considering the light in which he holds you. Never have I seen a man so proud of a daughter—or a son, either, for that matter."

"Aye?"

They were in the drawing room now and it seemed quite natural to Mike that in the yellow glow of candles the polished keys of a piano gleamed. She left him to pour wine at the sideboard and he, magnetized to the instrument, seated himself on the bench. He blinked wonderingly at the gold letters: Steinway, Chicago.

"They say," said Lady Marion, "that when I was born and he was told that I was a girl, he went away and did not return for months, so great was his grief at the misfortune." There was sadness lurking in her voice and she seemed to be speaking half to herself. She gave Mike a glass and clinked hers against his.

"To the Empire of England in the New World," she proposed.

"Nay," said Mike, swiftly. "I drink only to your beauty."

Lady Marion smiled and lowered her glass, while Mike drank his to the bottom against the necessity to answer her toast. Putting it aside, his fingers strayed to the ivory keys.

"Your father did not strike me as being such a foolish man," said Mike.

"He was not being foolish," said Lady Marion, spreading out her skirts as she sank down into a chair. "Who could carry on his business? Who could direct his ships upon the seas when he was gone? Nay, I understand. But for many years I did not. I could not know why he was so careless of me. But when my mother died he changed."

Mike's fingers caressed a musing chord from the instrument and it lingered in the room.

"He gave me presents after that. Funny presents like saddle horses and toy guns and a sailing boat. And because I was not yet nine I did not disagree, but played with them and enjoyed them. And when I would ride to hounds later on and take the brush before the first among the men, or when I would helm a boat to victory on the Thames in a race, or when I would down bags of birds with a fowling piece, he would be pleased. And because he was the only one I truly cared to please—for he's a darling old brigand—I developed what are strange skills in a woman."

"I would rather you called it fascinating," said Mike, playing softly a few bars from Brahms as a background to her lovely golden voice.

"Aye, my gallant sir. You would turn it to account. But women are not happy when they are able to beat men at their own games. When they can slap the face of a cad and have at him at dawn upon the field of honor, and yea, walk away from his quivering corpse."

"You've done that?" said Mike, the piano suddenly still.

"And worse. I'm useless to myself and to the world, sir. What is a woman but a wife? And how happy is a wife who has a man weaker than she?"

Mike's fingers drew out melody from the keys. "I can understand. In a time when women are supposed to be all froth and faint, the masculine accomplishments must set ill upon one so lovely."

"It is funny in a way," said Lady Marion. "I hope you forgive my statements and ha' no thought of my being an empty braggart, for these things to me are curses rather than accomplishments. Strange tastes for a lady. And how poor a sham am I. Tonight"—and her voice dropped a note and softened—"I almost was burst by my enthusiasm over your thrashing that vulgar hound, Braumley. I almost cheered my bravoes to you and shook your sword hand. But I tried to remember. I tried to be a lady. I turned and went away from men who would brawl before me. Of course, it was not your fault," she added, hastily. "But, as I say, sir, I am a counterfeit. No men dance with me. They salute me. No men send me flowers for fear they'll be returned in a nest of white feathers—aye, and vixen that I am, I've done, for I despise a coward. I am a lovely woman you say, sir, but I am a sham as a lady. Ah," and she sighed, "would that I *had* been born the boy my father wanted."

Mike looked at Lady Marion and found her sweet in her melancholy. There was strength in this woman as there is strength in a hunting leopard and there was also a straightforward attitude, a fearless ability to look any man in the eye which a seeking gallant might find very disconcerting. This, then, was the riddle of this woman. The loveliness of a siren and the courage and accomplishments of a knight. She had looked with longing upon men and had found them wanting. What strength and what ability the man must have who would at last win her affection—for she seemed afraid of giving that affection to any.

Mike strayed into Mendelssohn and, for a little time, lost them in the ecstatic depths of music. But he grew conscious at last of her eyes upon him, and his playing softened so that he could speak above it.

"He that would hold you would have the rarest jewel on earth, milady. Sorrow about yourself is like an oyster feeling badly about his pearl."

"I am told," she said, "that pearls are caused by a grain of sand irritating the oyster." And then she smiled. "I have told you of my woes. You have a right to tell yours."

"Ah, but you would not believe mine," said Mike. "You could not understand the story of a man trapped into a world quite foreign to him, playing a rôle which he does not understand, distrusting the reality of all things on earth and above, seeing no reason and having his own outraged, believing that all will fade too soon and grasping the fleeting instants of joy which, like gentle clouds hiding a scorching sun, too often and too swiftly blow away."

She was looking at him now, seeing him fully. And what a strange fellow she found him. A swordsman, better than an expert like Braumley, who could play better than anyone she had ever heard play, who could look like a king and talk like a poet.

Ah, yes, he was a very strange fellow. A strangely fascinating fellow. Here was not the straightforward bravery of Bristol, but the ultimate in gentility. Fearing weakness in her eyes, no man had ever played to her or said such fragile things to her before. But then, she sighed, there would be some flaw in him. There must be. There was in every other man. Some failing, perhaps a lack of courage in war or clearness in thought . . . With a start she realized that she had quite forgotten about Bristol, for a trumpet on the ramparts was even then beginning to bray of his approach.

Mike stopped playing and stood up. Far off they heard doors groan open and footsteps bang upon stone and iron and salutes from officers in the fort.

And then they heard, at the other end of the hall, the hoarse boom of Carstone's welcome.

Mike fingered the hilt of his sword.

Tom Bristol had come.

A coldly quiet voice was in conversation with Lord Carstone. Judging from the tones, the welcome speech had not been accepted and there seemed to be deadly business afoot. Lady Marion stood straighter, seemingly comprehending the situation perfectly; she advanced to the door and threw it open to go up the hall and into the room with her father and Bristol.

"My intelligences," said the clear, cold voice which evidently belonged to Bristol, "are quite different, sir."

"Aye, but damme, fellow, he's a guest!"

"Guest be damned, sir. I'll have a look at this don."

"He's no don," came Lady Marion's protest. "He's Irish."

"And perhaps, milady, a liar in the bargain," said Bristol, steadily.

Mike could not see them for they were in the dining salon. But he could see the guard, which had evidently come up with Bristol, and he liked the sight not at all. These brawny lads lounged in the corridor, whispering among themselves. They were sea-booted and clad in gay but stained jackets and half breeches and two of them wore headsilks, indicating that they were French. Swarthy and cruel of visage, they were quite obviously Brethren of the Coast, and the only thing which held their voices down was their presence here in the governor's fort and the fact that they were Bristol's escort. The eight of them in the corridor were complemented by five more in the balcony above the courtyard steps, five who guarded the offerings which Bristol had brought. Some twenty bearers, Maroons and Caribs, had eased down their heavy loads and now sat upon them awaiting further orders.

Mike did not know how it could be, but he recognized three of those Maroons. Tall, blade-faced fellows they were, not much darker than the English and French brethren and certainly cleaner and taller. Their names, those three, were Catshy, Zuil and Suyda. Mike was so intent upon his own danger that he took these things as they came and did not question. There were three fellows whom he had ordered flogged and thrown to the sharks, and yet—here they were. They knew him! Mike moved back from the door before he was seen. If he was clever about it, they'd never get a look at his face.

Meantime, the arguments raged and Captain Braumley's demands were added to Bristol's. "In the name of the crown, sir, we owe ourselves this much protection. If he is a Spanish officer and managed his escape, why, odds-bodikins! He'll carry back a complete record of the disposition of our forces and know our harbor and the ships in our fleets, and he'll know where he can land his troops! I say it's only fair that Bristol has a look at him."

"Aye," said Bristol. "Better now than to see him victor above a field of battle he has won by means of his inspection of this place. This, sir, is war!"

"Damme if you don't paint a gruesome picture of it, lad," said Carstone. "Well, peel your peepers at him, as you sailors say. But mind you don't try to act the boor that Braumley did." Carstone chortled, heavily. "Blind me, Captain, but you *did* look the clown, rolling down those steps!"

"Very well," said Bristol, "where is he?"

"In the drawing room," said the Lady Marion.

There was a sound of moving feet, and the buccaneers in the hall glanced at Bristol's face and loosened up their cutlasses in their bucklers and started to follow after.

"Stay!" said the Lady Marion. "Is this my home or a quarterdeck, sir?"

"Stand easy, lads," said Bristol. "The devil himself has never been known to fly."

The footsteps came on.

Mike stood beside the window, his face in dimness, his shadow painted gigantically upon an ancient tapestry by the guttering candles. His very first glimpse of Bristol told him that here was a man who would have to be removed if he himself was ever to be safe again.

Bristol was lean and hard. His handsome face was keen and strong. His eyes were as pale and cold as Arctic ice. He wore his own blond hair and it came in a metallic sweep down to the shoulders of his flaring cloak collar. There was a hard steel quality about the fellow which Mike felt would, in itself, turn the edge of a battle-ax.

"Michael O'Brien," said Lady Marion, "Captain Thomas Bristol. Captain Bristol, Michael O'Brien."

Mike bowed stiffly. Bristol nodded. Their eyes, since they had first seen each other, had caught and held and did not relax now for an instant. There was war in the atmosphere.

"I'm told," said Bristol, "that you were cast up by the sea after the wreck of a galleon. A fortunate escape."

"Aye," said Mike. "And from your bearers out there I suppose you to have had a successful voyage."

"Passing," said Bristol. "Would you like to look at the loot?"

The question was a trap to get him into the sight of those Maroons, Mike knew. And yet it seemed a good bait to grab.

"Why, yes, I wouldn't mind," said Mike. "How many ships and prisoners did you take, if I might ask?"

"Sufficient," said Bristol.

"A glass of wine, gentlemen?" said Lady Marion, putting glasses into their hands and pouring.

They drank without relaxing their vigils over each other. Carstone was uncomfortable and shuffled his feet and coughed. Braumley hovered just inside the door, ready for instant flight.

"The Spanish will weep when they hear of your success," said Mike.

"Aye. The English have wept too long," said Bristol.

---

"I might be persuaded to take one of your voyages with you," said Mike.

"I suppose you might," said Bristol. "And now, if you would like to look at the loot—" He turned to Carstone. "With your permission—"

But Carstone, while a good merchant, was not quick on his feet when it came to such subtle byplay. He mistook Bristol's design, or saw it not at all, for he said, "What? Look at it in the dark? Damme, Bristol, I thought you said that the presents—"

"Are yours, milord," said Bristol sharply in disappointment. "Have in the chests, Scudder!"

The word was passed and the Maroons and Caribs again took up their burdens to bring them into the drawing room and strew them over it. Mike stood with his face out of the light; Bristol had had no time to communicate his desire to the Maroons and so they withdrew without noticing the guest.

Bristol flung open a few chests and the candles made the jewels and gold pieces glitter and flame. He ran his hands through them and made them cascade back, letting some fall carelessly upon the carpet.

Carstone forgot all about this minor hostility and instantly began to open the rest of the chests and calculate their worth while Bristol stood back, still watching Mike. He seemed to find something deeper than a military menace in this stranger, for he was too brilliant, was Bristol, to fail to note that Lady Marion had sought to protect the fellow.

"And no prisoners for slaves?" said Carstone, at last. "We've acres upon acres untilled for want of labor. And if you ran across galleys, certainly you brought their oarsmen with you."

"No galleys," said Bristol. "Only prisoners of war."

"Bah!" said Carstone. "There's no such thing existing as a state of war. Spain and England and France are all at peace. How can they be prisoners of war? There are fields lying fallow and cane to be planted. And the weaklings they empty out of English jails die like rats from this damned fever."

Bristol seized upon that. He faced the door and called. "Scudder! Have in Zuil for a message to the ships!"

Presently the tall Maroon came. He was loose of movement, very free, almost regal, for his father was a cacique. His lemon-colored body was proudly wound about with bloodstained calico to hid the marks of the Spanish lashes.

He did not bow to the company, but nodded to his captain.

"Zuil," said Bristol. "We've a few prisoners on the *Fleetfoot* which his lordship would like to see. Have them brought up."

"Aye, aye," said Zuil.

But Bristol did not let him go and he cursed the man for not seeing the don there in the shadow. "Those on the *Fleetfoot*," he repeated. "Dons. And we regret that Miguel Saint Raoul de Lobo is not among them."

"Aye, we regret it," said Zuil, a little puzzled by this loquacity in one so usually taciturn.

"Have them up right away," said Bristol, nearly swearing.

Zuil turned and went away. Bristol angrily drained off another glass of wine as a toast to eventual success.

"Been long in these waters?" said Bristol.

"No," said Mike.

"Wonderful place," said Bristol.

"Aye," said Mike. "Wonderful."

"Except for the fever," said Bristol. "That gets the best of them."

"Aye, it must," said Mike.

Conversation languished as though words perished in this highly-electrified atmosphere. Several more glasses went the rounds and Carstone happily spent the time inspecting the spoils in detail. Bristol was getting madder by the minute, for a diamond necklace burned in his doublet to be clasped about the throat of Lady Marion. What a hellish homecoming! His eyes strayed to Mike continually and promised themselves compensation for this.

At last Zuil came back to say, "The prisoners are in the yard below, Captain."

Bristol sighed with relief. "We'll go out and look at them. All of us," said he. "And you, too, O'Brien, for you must see how low these dons can be reduced."

There was no refusing that without arousing further suspicion and so Mike trailed. He was somewhat startled to recognize his own hat, wide of brim and dark of plume, upon the piano as he passed, for he did not recall landing with a hat.

He put it on and drew it down to mask his features, and so got through the buccaneers and then the three Maroons he knew. The light was too bad and their suspicions too sleepy in this fort for them to take heed.

The prisoners were a mixed lot, many of them common sailors, battered and dirty and despairing; a few were soldiers and marines, stiffer but no less wretched. Two of them were officers, cloakless and swordless, but disdainful of their captors.

"Here they are, your lordship," said Bristol. "And a sorry lot they be."

"Aye, but slaves are scarce," said Carstone. And he started down at one end of the line, two boys bearing flambeaux beside him to light the yard, feeling muscles and looking at teeth, oblivious of the surly eyes of the captives. Carstone commented happily on each, calling off the faults.

The two Spanish officers were suddenly straighter and taller, but it was not they who betrayed Mike. He had lagged behind beside Lady Marion, listening to the chatter among the others.

And now, as they came to a mere child in the line, a ship's cadet from a gentle family, there was a sudden cry of gladness. Chains notwithstanding, the tiny cadet threw himself out of the line and at the feet of Mike.

"Almirante! Almirante! Save me!" And he gripped Mike's knee, weeping aloud, repeating, "Save me, Almirante!"

Mike kicked the child out of the way as gently as he could, but with speed. For down from the landing came the brethren, led by the three Maroons, and out from the scabbard leaped Bristol's rapier.

Stunned by his own activity, gripped, it seemed, by a gigantic power, dancing back with blade shrieking, Mike got the edge of the first Maroon. The Indian's cutlass went flying from the suddenly agonized hand, and Catshy was rolling over and over, pierced from navel to spine. There was a commotion in the line of prisoners, and then one of the officers had the cutlass and was breasting the tide which swept down the stairs. The flambeaux in the yard made it light below and shone into the eyes of the brawny lads coming down.

Mike was quite certain he was lost, for he could never stand these devils off with the help of just one officer!

*Clank!*

The prisoners had all been chained together, but now there was a shift. Each one was miraculously chained independently in such a way that he would be wielding his fetters as a weapon!

Lady Marion screamed and Mike whipped about to find himself faced by Bristol. Their weapons engaged with fury, and then Bristol was suddenly yanked down from behind by the Spaniards and Mike whirled back to the steps in time to help block the rush of buccaneers.

It was a seething maelstrom of blades and cloaks, but it was brief. Soldiers up on the battlements were streaming down to join the fray, and these, too, had the disadvantage of having to come down narrow stairs, for the slaves-to-be had heavy wrist chains which they used to deadly purpose, crushing skulls and limbs at every sweep.

Over a courtyard slippery with blood and brains, Mike rushed to the gates, crying the Spaniards after him in their tongue. The flambeaux bearers had been ground underfoot, and the only light came from a moonless sky and a faraway harbor, and then from flaming powder. The furious volley splashed the courtyard redder still and the balls whined by or thudded into bodies.

"The gate!" bellowed Mike. *"La puerta!"*

The three chained gangs of Spaniards sought to follow. One of them, the farthest away, flayed the soldiers with such ferocity that even it won through. Another volley crashed and along the chains could be felt dead weights. Dragging their wounded and corpses alike, married to them by iron links, the Spaniards came up to Mike.

Four soldiers had surged from the sentinel boxes to stop the escape. The only light here was a lantern's dim beams, and it showed them a tall demon with a naked, dripping rapier in a lace-cuffed hand. Two knelt to fire, two drew.

Mike faced those guns with horror. At point-blank range even a muzzle-loading musket could not miss! And those two tunnels were lined upon his breast as true as though laid by a transit. And the linstocks were raised to the touch-holes, and in a moment Mike would be torn to shreds!

*Clank!*

He had a steel corselet about him which he had not had before. He made a mental note to thank Hackett and even as he acted had a sudden chill of knowing that so far something had always happened to save him, but that he could not possibly continue to depend upon it. The hero, Bristol, might. But not Mike, the villain of the piece!

Mike's rapier tore out the throat of a soldier who had drawn and nearly in the same movement punctured the other where his belts crossed whitely.

And then another fighter blocked the way—Bristol! He threw himself at Mike with an icy fury and a strength which would have thrown down soldiers or sailors like empty bottles. But Mike caught the hilt of the other's blade with his own hilt and they stayed there, locked, pressing, faces but inches apart.

"You Spanish hellion!" snarled Bristol. "I'll never rest until I see you swing! In the eyes of the English, you'll be nothing but a spy from now until the day you're dead!"

"I'm not a pirate," said Mike through his teeth.

"God's blood, I'll have your heart for that!"

"And I," said Mike, "will probably have your Lady Marion. Out of the way, gutter sweepings!"

The gangs of Spaniards had halted for an instant but now they swept over Bristol and battered him under and went racing through the gates.

Mike groped for a moment in the dark, for a ball had extinguished the lantern. He found the corpse of a soldier and grasped his powder horn. From another, a cannoneer who had rushed down from the walls, he snatched a burning linstock.

Then to the gang of Spaniards who waited for him he cried, "Shut the gates!"

Musketry was going from the inner fort but most of the soldiers had leaped up the walls in an attempt to sweep the

Spaniards from the road below. Balls snapped about Mike and thudded into the wood of the gate. A squad was making a rush for the portals and Mike narrowly missed being cut off from his men. He got the gate closed with Spaniard help and then emptied the horn at the foot of it, trailing the powder after him as he leaped back. He dropped the linstock's spark into the chain. There was a puff and then a swift sweep of greenish flame which raced back to the pile and swooped upwards along each edge of the nearly closed doors. These, being of wood and subjected to such terrific heat, caught and blazed.

Mike, balls thudding all about him, sped after his rescued troops. Not yet was the light behind bright enough to show up the whole road and in an instant they had turned the bend and were on the steep part of the trail which led to the town.

Mike urged them on when he reached them. They were shadows against the lighter dark and for a moment he could not understand the dragging sound which went with them, or what cut down their flight. And then he trod upon a wounded man being dragged along by the others attached to his chain.

"*Alto!*" said Mike. "Captain, your cutlass here, sir."

It was gruesome and bloody work, cutting the corpses out of that chain, severing limbs which were less resistant to a blade than iron. Only two of the wounded were able to stagger along with help. The others, knowing what lay behind them in English hands, begged for death, not abandonment.

And then Mike, about to order that death much to his own horror, changed that order. "Pick them up, you hulks. Are we English?"

They burdened themselves with the wounded.

The sound of the typewriter faded to nothing.

The burning gate and the musket fire had attracted attention in the town and now buccaneers and some of the soldiers of the customs house came struggling up the hill through the hot night to investigate, arming themselves about with swords and pistols as they came.

But their hurry was too great for torches.

"Into the brush!" said Mike.

The Spaniards dodged under the bushes and crouched there while the men streamed up. But Mike stood on the side of the road, crying, "Hurry! It's been attacked by the Spanish from the hills! Hurry!"

They hurried. And after three or four minutes the road was wholly clear. Mike led them down, straight upon the town. Behind them on the hill could be heard shouts and further firing, for the English had evidently concluded that if they had not been upon the road, then they had taken the trail to the beach which flanked the castle.

The buccaneers, heavy with pay and lust, had been well begun upon the evening and those who could still walk had hurried to the castle's "defense." It was easy to get through the town. Drunken songs rolled out of the taverns, inert men lay in the gutters. The Spaniards were armed when they reached the dock. They threw themselves into long-boats and despite their chains, managed to row. The lights of the tallest ship attracted them, making a yellow pathway to them. And when they neared it they were again entertained by loud and bawdy verses from "The Grave at Gaverley" and "The Mermaid." After the custom of the brethren there was no discipline in port and this, the ship guard itself, was slopping with brandy to the point that they did not decry a boat or offer it salute.

The longboats came in alongside the main ladder and Mike leaped up. The deck was badly lighted but he could see men gaming and drinking on a tarpaulin over a hatch. They, in turn, did not see him against the blackness. Other men slept in the squat shadows of guns, empty pots beside them. Mike waved up his Spaniards and it was not until their chains clanked upon the deck itself that they were seen.

The gamblers stared round-mouthed at these tatterde-malions and at the steadily held pistols in their hands.

Mike looked them over and said, "Ye'll make much better slaves alive than dead. Raise a voice and we'll let it out of the side of your throats. Captain Fernando, find the carpenter's chest and an anvil. Those chains are a mite too heavy for the rigging. Lieutenant Rescate, clap these beggars under hatches. And now where's the cadet that gave it away?"

"He's dead, Almirante," said a soldier.

Mike walked over to the gunwale and looked steadily at the fort on the hill.

He walked aft and up to the quarterdeck and still stared at it.

When the sails were shaking out in the light evening wind, Mike again gave his attention to the boat. He had the lights knocked out and with his helmsmen alert, began the task of working quietly past the fort, tense with the knowledge that they might receive a withering cannonade from there, darkness or no darkness.

He stood back, detached from himself, and heard strange terms issue from his lips. Not only was he giving the proper nautical orders, but also he was giving them in Castilian!

He could not speak Spanish but he was speaking Spanish! He knew nothing about boats and yet with masterful ease he was sailing one of a type three centuries vanished from the deeps!

Could this be Mike, man about town, dilettante of the arts?

And how strange it was to find this all so common to himself! Here he had killed seven or eight men in twenty-four hours more or less, had engineered an escape from a fortress, had met the deadliest enemy he would ever have, was in command of a vessel of war and—and—could it be, now that he thought of it?—fallen in love with the loveliest woman he had ever seen in any picture or any clime.

Could that have been Mike—Michael de Wolf—who doffed his hat so grandly and drew so wickedly and spoke with such gallantry and poise?

What strange power was this which decreed all these things?

They worked their way past the snoring fort and stood out from the island with the east trades sighing in the hemp and canvas aloft.

"Starboard a point," said Mike.

"Steady," said Mike.

Tall masts against the stars, cool wind against his cheek, the restive but soothing breast of the sea . . . What lay ahead of him now? He had heard himself set the course for Nombre de Dios. Did such a place exist?—though part of him seemed to know that it did and even recalled how it looked.

And there—certainly they'd know him for a fraud.

Almirante Miguel Saint Raoul de Lobo, commanding his most Catholic majesty's fleets in the New World, commissioned to seek out and destroy the English and the French, pitted against buccaneers who fought like hop-headed wild cats and drank like barrels, pitted against Captain Tom Bristol, the coolest and toughest and cleverest of them all!

Mike shuddered and wrapped his beautiful cloak more tightly about him. The shadow of the helmsman showed up against the dully glowing binnacle. The soft hiss of sea came from under the *Fleetfoot*'s stern. The long white wake faded into the dark behind and the path of a star reached out to them before.

"She's luffing her t'ps'ls," said Mike. "Bring the breeze farther astern."

Had he said that?

How did he know?

How—Wh—

WHY?

And how would all this end?

# CHAPTER
## SIX

Nombre de Dios was a sweat-soaked town, fried by sun, steamed by jungle, depopulated by fever, commanded by a martinet, shaken by earthquakes, worked by slaves and cluttered with great stacks of silver and gold.

Once there had been two-storied houses here, but the earthquakes had taught the Spaniards better. Once there had been Maroons in the jungle behind, but those who were not dead and who had not been chained into the work gangs on the docks and in the forts had prudently taken themselves far back into the tangled hills. Once this had been a quiet curve of the shore; now it was the shipping point of all the gold which came by mule train across the Isthmus and from here sailed the mighty plate fleet, carrying, ship by ship, a ransom which would have bought Caesar.

There was yellow jack and malaria. There were scorpions and centipedes. There were bright parrots and chattering monkeys. There were masts in the shipyard and gay shawls upon the low balconies. There were Spanish soldiers in bright yellow uniforms, Spanish sailors in tasseled caps and striped shirts, black slaves in hoarsely rattling chains, grand ladies in carriages, dogs in sunlight, potbellied Indian children snoozing in the shade, mules with silken-covered saddles or gay panniers, rowboats on blue water, fortress battlements against blue sky—and over it all the golden banner of Castile and Leon.

When the great golden trains came with their inconceivable wealth, merchants and Indians and gentlemen and ladies jammed the town's thin streets, but they did not linger, for lingering might be as expensive as one's life—such was the fever.

Mike sat in a long chair, cooling his hand with a drink. From this silk-canopied balcony stretched the town, swooping away down the hill to the harbor.

For the first month Mike had been fascinated by the intricacy of this place, by the brutality shown slaves, by the gagging reality of yellow jack, by the whole mad colorful picture of Spanish life in the New World. But now Mike was bored. For another month he had languished. Little by little he had brought up seemingly concrete memories of his past. Without hesitation, he recognized people and called them by their right names and inquired properly after their children. But he had lived in a state of dread lest they suddenly discover that he was Mike de Wolf, not Miguel Saint Raoul de Lobo, lord and almirante. Now that dread had nearly vanished, for one and all they found him wholly credible and were most bowingly polite—all except one called Father Mercy and another, Lord Bagatela, governor of all this and captain of its forces.

Father Mercy was so repulsive that Mike had been at much trouble not to be found alone with him. And Lord Bagatela was such a dismal bore with his tales of the last war and how he had won it for his most Catholic majesty—practically singlehanded—and so jealous of the sweeping authority Mike had from that most Catholic majesty's hand, that Mike was made most uncomfortable by him.

Only one man seemed to be impossible to shake and that was Trombo. He was a gigantic creature with a blankly relaxed face, a small pin-pointed head with no brow at all and an arm which could crush the life out of a man with one squeeze. Trombo went about clad in dirty white pants, his bare chest agleam with greasy sweat. He had no hair upon him and was a shade of bright yellow, as though he had been painted thickly.

Trombo never, for one instant, let Mike out of his sight. And Mike had protested, but, "Almirante señor, once I let you go and you were almost killed. When next the barbarian English touch you, Trombo shall be there and Trombo's great sword shall make the heads fly." Here came a dreamy expression, like a child lushing up an ice-cream soda on a hot day. "Ah yes, Almirante señor, and the blood will spatter about like rain. Rain!" He laughed soundlessly and added, "and the other English will think maybe Mount Pelée had exploded again! I, Trombo, shall teach them not to touch my almirante!"

That was that and there he sat, knees drawn up to his chin, fondly regarding his admiral. It was enough to give a man screaming nightmares!

There were some divergencies from the usual in the scene which had at first made Mike's mind reel but which he now accepted—being unable to do anything else. Monkeys chattered incessantly, night and day, and parrots screamed without rest. There were women in the streets who seemed to have no function but to parade endlessly, never stopping anywhere. The sea and the sky were never anything but blue—when seas are usually every shade in the spectrum at various times.

Mike had been able to come to a definite conclusion regarding his predicament. He had no doubt that this was "Blood and Loot," by Horace Hackett, and that the whole panorama was activated only by Horace Hackett's mind. And what Horace Hackett said was so, was so. And what Horace Hackett said people said, they said. And when Horace Hackett said that the almirante waited two months for the repair of his gale-battered fleet and the arrival of ships from Spain to augment it, then the almirante did nothing for two months but wait.

And if Horace Hackett forgot to complete a scenic effect, then it was incomplete. But if he generalized and said this was Nombre de Dios of 1640, then it *was* Nombre de Dios of 1640, with all the trimmings and the people. And if he said it was an ever-blue sea, then, b'god, the sea was bluish even at night.

And if Horace Hackett stated that the parrots and monkeys screamed and chattered endlessly, so they did. And if women paraded continually, they paraded continually.

Mike understood now that the whole story ran in one limitless scene which continued in all places together. But the scene of the story in particular shifted from spot to spot, from character to character, so that men were become puppets of the pen and, realizing it not at all, were put through actions to suit the plot. Mike knew now that he must have been described early in "Blood and Loot" as an accomplished swordsman, a talented sailor, and brilliant strategist, for it would be like Horace to make his villains good and strong, the more to baffle the hero. Under the invisible spotlight of Horace's genius, Mike had carried through the situations splendidly. But it was somehow horrible suddenly to begin to talk in stilted English or Spanish, to become poised and gallant and deadly and to be swept along by a force which was wholly invisible and untouchable.

Mike had found himself, upon his arrival at Nombre de Dios, spending a great deal of time thinking about the Lady Marion and sighing for her company. It was real and deep and hurtful and it made his nights restless.

Then Mike, pondering, had brought himself to face the fact that this love for the Lady Marion was a part of the plot and that if he succumbed to that feeling, why, then he was inevitably doomed. He knew how Horace Hackett plotted. Lady Marion would attract him. He would raid an English island in an attempt to carry her off. Bristol would be infuriated beyond reason by the success of the attempt and would move hurricanes to get at him and have the lady back. And that would be the end of Mr. Almirante Miguel de Lobo, spitted like a chicken upon Tom Bristol's lightning blade.

This, for a space, nearly smothered his love for milady. But in his dreams he kept seeing her and at times like this his boredom tricked him into thinking fondly of her. And the first thing he knew he was furious with Tom Bristol for being the hero of this tale, for eventually getting the lady, for eventually stabbing the almirante.

There was a bare chance that Horace might break down and make a tragedy out of this thing and if so, then it would be Tom Bristol who would die and the Lady Marion would be Mike's and all would be well. But that could not be depended upon.

Mike saw his fate laid out in the neat pattern of Horace's plot. Already he had seen men die in agony upon this scene. Already he had drunk the blood of human beings with his rapier. And he did not doubt, when he found at last that he did not return to his own world, that he would meet his complete end behind the pages of "Blood and Loot." Horace Hackett, all unwittingly, would murder his friend. And Mike disliked the idea of dying, not only horribly, but completely defeated and disgraced. No, it was not probable that he would get out of this story. And the hell of it was that this story was real—figment of Horace's imagination or not.

Wouldn't he like to tell Horace a thing or two now! Batting him on the head, caving in his side—were those polite things to do to your best friend? He could imagine Horace sitting there—dirty bathrobe swathed about his rotundity, half-empty coffee cup full of dead butts—being wittily incredulous.

And the more Mike thought about it, the madder he got. And the more he tried to forget her, the more he loved the Lady Marion.

Nights he lay twisting about on sweat-soaked sheets, cursing his luck and fate.

And just now, sitting on his shaded balcony, calm of face but mentally a-boil, Mike de Wolf planned revolt.

He'd show this Horace Hackett a thing or two. He'd take this story into his own hands!

He knew how it went, or could guess at it. How much time he had he did not know, for he understood that time in the world and time here were two different things—for here Horace merely had to say "three months went by," and so they did, day dragging after day, whereas it took only a second or two to hammer out those four words on the typewriter. It was possible then for him to get together a fleet that would really be a fleet and wipe the English and French out of these islands by an attack nothing could stop. It was also possible for him to refuse to take the field against Tom Bristol at all, but he knew that if he remained inert then Bristol would come for him.

"You bothered," said Trombo, with the air of one announcing the solution to months of high-gear mental effort.

"Why?" said Mike.

"You no see Zuilerma at all. She cry and not leave her room and say she is grown too old for her almirante. She not yet eighteen. Why you not like her?"

Mike gave a slight shudder. Usually Trombo talked decent Spanish, but now he spoke bad English. Evidently Horace Hackett had shifted his spotlight for a moment to Nombre de Dios. All right, let him shift it.

To hell with Horace Hackett.

He, Mike de Wolf, wouldn't talk!

"Letters come from Panama," said Trombo, stubbornly. "Anne write and write and write and say why the almirante no send escort for her? She say she is not afraid of the fever here if it means she can see her almirante. She say she dead with worry about you and why you not write her."

Still no answer from Mike. He felt a small thrill of triumph. He could keep from talking! Even though this was an obviously posed scene.

"You in love," said Trombo with finality.

"What?" cried Mike. "Nonsense!"And he was instantly sorry, for he doubted then his ability to run this scene.

"You in love. Fifty-'leven most beautiful women in New World die for sight of you and you in love. Why not whistle? Almirante whistle, any woman on earth run to him. He is the almirante! He is beautiful!"

"I want no women," said Mike.

"You in love," said Trombo. "You think I blind? You say what woman and Trombo take ship and get her and bring her back. Not good for you to love woman. You take her, you forget about her."

"You're treading on swampy ground, Trombo."

"You walking into fever if you not perk up. If you not think Trombo better go get this woman, then let Trombo go get Anne. Or send for Zuilerma. Or buy twenty-thirty slave girl. Or make love to governor's wife. She almost die whenever she look on you, and she plenty young and a great lady, too. Who you want you can have. You are the almirante! You are beautiful!"

"Stop it," said Mike. "Do you think if I actually wanted a woman I would not take her?"

"Well? Then why not take this one?"

"She—she is a long way away. And—she is English."

"*English!*" cried Trombo, leaping up in horror.

"Aye," said Mike, quietly. "She is the Lady Marion Carstone, the sweetheart of Captain Bristol."

"The—the sweetheart of a pirate!" cried Trombo. "Oh, oh, oh, the almirante has been too much in the sun. The fever has him!" He held his head in his hands and rocked as though in pain.

"And," said Mike, quietly, "I intend to have her as a prisoner of war."

Trombo stopped. The despair went slowly from his face, to be replaced by pleasure. "This Captain Bristol, he is a terrible name on the Main now. He has a big fleet but the almirante will stop him. Ah, ah, ah! To defeat him, to yardhaul him! To cut out his guts before his eyes and feed them to a dog! And to take his woman— Ah, that is revenge great enough even for the almirante! Ah, ah, my almirante, forgive me. I am blind. You are quiet because you plan this!"

"Aye," said Mike, aghast at feeling pleasure from such a gruesomely stated picture.

"Why—why, even Zuilerma can see sense in that!" cried Trombo. "When you have become bored with the English woman you can give her to Zuilerma and Zuilerma will be pleased. She is clever with a knife, is Zuilerma—"

"No!" cried Mike. "I really love the Lady Marion, Trombo."

"Ah, love, pah! I saw you in love with fifty-'leven women. You take 'em, you get bored, you forget 'em. There is Zuilerma. You heard of her beauty and fought and killed full two hundred Indians to capture her. And now you bored. You spend nights risking fever with a guitar under Anne's window and now she begs you let her come to you and you not answer letters."

"This is different," said Mike severely.

There was rebuke in the tone and so Trombo became silent. But the certainty of knowledge did not die from his face. He knew his almirante and he felt much better about the whole thing.

All that had to be done, would be done.

But a grey shadow drifted over the shining hardwood floor and it was not to be as simple as that. Father Mercy had come in like a pallbearer, even more grizzly than ever. He had, quite obviously, been eavesdropping.

"My son," said Father Mercy, "I have come to pay a call."

"Delighted, father," said Mike. "Sit down."

"What I have to say I would rather say standing up, my son." And his corpse face remained still, lips unmoving though he spoke. "I have dissuaded the sale of English captives ever since you have known me, my son."

Mike looked at him insolently and sipped his drink. He felt a strong repulsion for this horror of a man, one that was not born out of Hackett. And so strong was it that Mike momentarily slipped away from the grip upon him.

"You soul-scavenging buzzard," said Mike. "When I pulled into this harbor you damned near had the town upside down, telling people that I ought to give you the captives I took. Well, to hell with you. They're English and they're men and if you crave autos-da-fé every day, use up Indians and leave white men alone. They're at the fort now, working. And I have them counted every day. And the first one that is missing will find me shelling that hell hole you call a religious prison! Now get out of here!"

Father Mercy gaped. "My son—they are heretics! The rack and the Iron Maiden alone can extract their sins. It is the only way to get them to believe and save their souls."

"Kill a man to save his soul. What's so damned valuable about a soul, you crow? Why tear a man's body to bits and send him to his God in chunks? I've a packet of orders in that strong box there which empower me above church and state and if I so decree it, they empower me above God as well so far as you are concerned. You and your sadistic lechery ought to be wiped out of this town like I'd squash a centipede."

"Have a care, my son. I am a man of God, and as such I am more powerful in my influence than you in yours. These statements which you have made can, perhaps, be overlooked, though I have never had to listen to such blasphemy before." And indeed, Father Mercy was shivering under emotional stress. "Just now I happened to overhear your designs upon an English girl. I came in to again demand the souls of those English you captured and I stay to demand that all English heretics landed here shall become the charges of our church. And this girl, too, must be delivered like the rest. The governor, Lord Bagatela, has just now said that he cannot give them up without your permission and I have just told Lord Bagatela that I am about to report the matter to Spain via the first advice boat—and you cannot touch religious mails. Unless you promise this thing, I shall use every power of the church to have you removed from command and given over to our care, for now your blasphemy tempts me to report above all else. However, if you give me these captives and if you promise me this"—he swallowed hard—"English woman, you are safe."

"Feed white flesh to your damned racks?" cried Mike. "I'll blow this town off the map first and I've got the ships and guns to do it."

"You cannot force the hand of God, sir."

"God?" said Mike, suddenly thinking upon the true identity of this priest's god and vividly envisioning Horace Hackett. "God, did you say? Your god, sir priest, is as lecherous as thou. Now go and cease to drag your dirt on my floor!"

"Blasphemy!" chattered the priest. "You—you are mad!" And he expected the heavens to cave in on him. "B-b-blasphemy!" And he fled with skirts streaming behind him from out of this ghastly presence.

Mike laughed and Trombo shuddered.

"Love," muttered Trombo, "*has* driven you mad, Almirante. Father Mercy will have you racked! And his report to Spain cannot be touched. You are *mad*." And he wept.

# CHAPTER SEVEN

**M**ad or not, Almirante Miguel Saint Raoul de Lobo set sail from Nombre de Dios with bands playing, pennons streaming and the gilded hulls of his galleons and round ships majestically reflected in the water. He was escorting the plate fleet past the leeward islands and the hands of his cannoneers itched to apply the linstock to the touchhole with English buccaneers as a target.

Mike, for all his outward decision, was fighting a mighty battle within himself. How he ached to attack St. Kitts as soon as this plate fleet was safely into the Atlantic! And why shouldn't he? He knew the defenses and the channel. He knew the positions of the forts and the disposition of the troops and very nearly could guess the number of vessels which would be on hand. To attack and take and if

Buccaneer Bristol was not among the slain or the captives, then to hold the Lady Marion as hostage against future behavior—that was the indicated plan and one in which he was certain he could succeed.

But Mike had slightly the edge of these other denizens of Never-never Land. While they were quite human and much alive and while they supposed themselves in a world quite as concrete as the world from which Mike had come, they were not on talking terms with their deity. And Mike knew every plot twist of which Horace Hackett was capable. And he knew that even though this looked so neat, there must be something wrong with it. His captains had already mentioned its feasibility and had advised its operation. Even Father Mercy, with the prospect of putting a fair English lass upon the rack, argued austerely that it was good colonial policy. Aye, Mike told himself, there was something damned wrong with it if the others had all thought of it.

Sailing six points from the wind to beat through Mona Passage and ride the Gulf Stream to the Old World, the transports waddled along, bellies deep in the sea with riches. Striding the twenty paces up and down his quarterdeck on the *Josef y Maria*, Mike recalled, one by one, Horace Hackett's previous tales. Porpoises rolled along beside the ship, flying fish flashed in fright away from the white-toothed bows, sails to port, starboard and astern blazed white and red and gold against the achingly hot sky. Mike turned and turned again, soft white boots making little sound above the sigh of wind.

This world was so *real* to those who lived in it. They lived and were born and they got sick and felt pain and died. And they looked up into the blue, wholly unconscious that they might well hear the rattling of a typewriter's keys and smell the horrible pipe which Horace Hackett clenched in yellow teeth. From whence had this world come, whither would it go? These people all thought they remembered long pasts and ancestors. They were convinced that their progeny would continue up the ages. They believed in their ingenuity and trusted their calculations. And yet—

Mike could never remember a story in which Horace Hackett had refrained from killing his villain. The hero triumphed, got the girl and slaughtered the evil one.

Well, Mike was the "evil one," but he did not care about being slaughtered.

"If I could only figure it out," muttered Mike. "If I could turn this plot and get Bristol—" Yes, there was a chance, for Horace Hackett was not always concerned with each scene simultaneously. Right now, sailing along, Mike knew that he was free from Hackett's direction. And being free, he could talk as he pleased and act as he pleased and—

Supposing—supposing he did not wind up at St. Kitts. Supposing he went somewhere else and when Horace had the attack all figured out for St. Kitts, the Spanish fleet was some hundreds of miles hence!

Mike grinned.

The ships swept grandly onwards.

He would control this strange love for the Lady Marion. He would refuse to fall into such an obvious trap. He would wipe the English from the Main and leave Tom Bristol much alone. Aye!

Hell, now he was doing it by himself.

Aye.

Accordingly, some days later the naval vessels hauled yards and while their brilliant canvas fluttered from luff to leech, dipped their flags in salute to the onward-surging round ships. The long Atlantic swell made their gun tackles creak and jumped pans off the galley stoves, but they lay in the trough for an hour to make certain that the plate fleet was out on the broad highway, unpursued by buccaneers, headed for Spain with the Caribbean far behind. They wore ship then and, forming a long line, braced and steadied for Mona Passage.

"It might be easier," said Fernando in the chart room, "to stand out and come down on St. Kitts with the wind aquarter."

Mike's compass poised over the crudely drawn parchment chart which showed things as though the view was from above the horizon and not the zenith.

He looked at Fernando.

"Perhaps," said Mike, "we'll not attack St. Kitts."

"But—but I thought your orders, sire—"

"My orders are most general, Captain. I am supposed to wipe out the English and there is more than one English settlement in the New World."

"But I had heard—That is, the rumor had it—"

"That a woman was involved?"

"Something like that, sire."

Mike grinned. "Fernando, have you ever thought much on destiny?"

"Why—no, sire. The church—"

"Destiny is a marvelous thing. Circumventing destiny is possible only by refusing to do the obvious."

This seemed like blasphemy to Fernando and he remained silent.

"Strategy is of the same stuff," said Mike. "Men are lifted into key positions, they know not why. They strive and fail or succeed, still not knowing why. They have the breaks or they have not the breaks. But, in a limited scope, they can determine their own futures."

It certainly did sound like blasphemy, but Fernando, in obedience to his almirante, nodded.

"And so," said Mike, "you will issue orders to officers commanding the rest of the fleet to the effect that we are proceeding not to St. Kitts, but a place much nearer to us—Tortuga."

"But—why?"

"There is an English and French settlement there. There will be vessels there which could ultimately aid Bristol in attacking our towns and colonies. It is the buccaneering hotbed of the Caribbean—and if we have any luck, the buccan hunters will all be out leveling their sights upon wild steers while we level ours upon their settlement. We will land and destroy the place—with all due humanity, of course—and we'll burn what ships we find there, thus weakening Bristol's future fleet. Then if Bristol attacks, what men he would normally get from Tortuga will be safely inside our prisons or quietly dead."

"Why—that's brilliant!" said Fernando. "And that woman—I mean in St. Kitts—Father Mercy was wrong in saying that you—"

"There are spies. All Indians are spies. Perhaps, Captain, that was a remark calculated to disturb the peace of mind on St. Kitts and make our attack on Tortuga simple. Perhaps."

Fernando beamed with admiration. And then, "The course, sire?"

"West sou-west, b'half south," said Mike. "Locate a sea-artist in our fleet who has been in there and have him come aboard the flagship here as pilot."

"Si, si, Almirante," said Fernando and hurried away from the cabin.

Mike sat contemplating the chart before him. He was not particularly amazed anymore by these sudden abilities of his. First as a swordsman, then as a linguist. And now out of the clear he found himself a naval strategist. But he wasn't giving it much thought. He was too pleased with himself for having bested his own desires and having turned the tables on one Horace Hackett.

Tortuga, so named because, as now, it looked like a gigantic turtle's back awash in the sea, hove up with the dawn. A silent fleet was coasting along Haiti's north at two knots, banners but half seen from ship to ship in the mist.

Mike stood in the great cabin of the *Josef y Maria* and addressed his captains who had gathered from the ships for his orders. They sat quietly drinking their morning coffee, their aristocratic faces without trace of concern for the forthcoming battle. Mike, booted and cloaked for action, paced up and down the great stained-glass stern ports as he spoke, the sun coming up to silhouette him in the scarlet flame of dawn.

"The ships will attack as outlined," concluded Mike. "The landing parties will get away as soon as the harbor vessels are smashed and these will take the forts as I have outlined. But I wish to make one thing clear to you, gentlemen. We are captains and sailors of his most Catholic majesty's navy and we will conduct ourselves as such. There will be no ravishing of this town. There will be no useless slaughter. We are here on a military objective and civilians are not fair game. I will enforce this order with all the authority at my command."

The captains looked wonderingly at one another, for after all, weren't these people of Tortuga English and French? But orders were orders and they nodded politely, drained their coffee and went on deck to call for their boats. In a short time they were aboard their own vessels. In an hour the *Josef y Maria*'s prow was thrusting past the earthworks of eastern Tortuga, while the leading ship of the other line readied to blast out the fortresses of the Haitian shores.

The battle flag on Mike's flagship dipped.

A rolling broadside shook the very sea. White smoke whirled out to darken the mists. The trumpeters of the fleet knifed the morning with their calls and signals. The marines rapped out a hysterical background to the cannon with their muskets.

The forts on either side of the channel were churned vales of flying masonry from which scrambled men who sometimes almost got away.

The Spanish raid on Tortuga had begun.

Six hours later the battle was over.

The anchorage had been but sparsely populated with ships, except for fifteen merchantmen which had put in there for food and stores and some twelve buccaneer craft which were undergoing, for the most part, overhaul. The merchantmen had gaped at the Spanish fleet in all its flaming glory and had struck almost to a man, but the buccaneer vessel, even though careened and in no position whatever to give resistance, knew that even a small fight was better than no fight and an end on a Spanish gibbet. These latter ships had fought furiously if unavailingly to oppose the landing on the island. They were now blazing wrecks filled with roasting corpses.

Tortuga had been attacked at an unfortunate time—for Tortuga. Its inhabitants combined the trade of hunting and curing meat with raiding on the Main and at this season nearly the entire male population was deep into Spanish Haiti, drumming up the wild beef which had, over the years, retreated to higher ground away from the coast. Accordingly, there were very few in the forts—only those who had been hurriedly rushed there to man the cannon upon the first appearance of the Spanish. Shot and powder had been fed the guns in some cases by women and children and these were now dead in the rubble.

A few of the houses on the island offered the appearance of fortresses and these were shelled heartily by the Spanish ships before Mike could pass the order.

A company not more than a hundred strong had drawn a battle line upon the sand to oppose the landing of five hundred Spanish marines. And now the sand was a dark, thick red. Onward had swept the landing party, to cut off the retreat of men from the forts and shortly after, the golden banner of Castile and Leon was flowing over Tortuga.

Six hours and the battle was over.

Mike had recall sounded. But in the din ashore it might as well have been whispered. Mike had the other vessels signaled, but no signalmen answered. The anchorage lived with longboats filled with Spaniards. The jungle behind the town moved with yellow-jacketed marines. A signal gun bidding them return to their ships went unnoticed.

Too long had these Spaniards lost to the buccaneer to show mercy now. And the sky began to blacken with the smoke of burning buildings, mingling with the smoke of charring ships. With cutlass and crossbow, musket and lance, the population of Tortuga was being slaughtered to the last child.

As soon as he realized what was happening, Mike rallied the crew of the *Josef y Maria* which was still aboard, poured them and his marines into the boats and drew them up on the beach. At their head he set out to quell this madness. But a hundred yards into the town his men thinned, dribbling away one by one, hungry after loot and wine and death and Mike was left upon the smoking street, alone save for Trombo.

With the flat of his sword and the might of Trombo's arm, Mike sought to stop the massacre. Women fled from doorways to be seized or struck down before they could cry out. The drunken marines flung all possessions from the homes and ripped them apart, searching for valuables. They could not hear Mike's voice. Old men and priests were being tortured to discover the hiding of money in the hills.

The place was a howling shambles with walls caving in, smoke everywhere, screams of agony and wails for quarter on all sides. Dead and wounded sprawled in the dust. And sailors and marines rushed on in search of more loot, more women, more brandy and rum. Five thousand devils in yellow and blue gutting the hearts from Tortuga's twenty thousand women, children and old men.

Mike, sweating and furious, laid about him with his rapier, powerless to bring any men to recognize him—and failing, in his anger spitted them and slashed them down. But it was for nothing that Trombo strove so mightily with him, and by midafternoon Mike gave it up, sinking down upon a stone step of a house not yet burned, holding his head in his hands, sick with the horror of it and the realization of what he had loosed.

"They mad and drunk," said Trombo, trying vainly to understand why the thing had to be stopped. "Tomorrow they listen to you."

"Tomorrow!" cried Mike. "Tomorrow there won't be a thing alive on Tortuga."

"They all English and French," shrugged Trombo.

---

"I'll court-martial the whole fleet!" vowed Mike. "I'll have them under hatch all the way to Nombre de Dios. I'll string them up by their thumbs and yard haul them and—and—" He relapsed into apathy.

Trombo suspected sunstroke as the cause of this strange mental quirk and he sought about for something to quench his almirante's thirst and take his mind from the crew's disobedience. Of course a man is always angry, thought Trombo, when his men refuse to obey him. He looked up at the white walls of this so far spared home. It was bigger than most and it ought to be richer. Gold and good wine whetted Trombo's appetite. He made sure his almirante was all right, and then, throwing his shoulder against the door with all his mighty strength, caved the portal as though it had been built of sand.

Mike lifted his head from his hands and wondered where Trombo had gone. He shouted for him once or twice but he could not hear his own voice in the bedlam of the town. He turned and saw that the door of the place was open and, suspecting, got up to look in. Almost immediately he found Trombo. The giant was carrying a flagon of brandy, which he proudly set down and from which he poured a drink for his almirante.

Past them, from the street, dashed several sailors who instantly went about the work of ransacking the place for money and jewels, paying no heed in their drunken eagerness to Mike.

And a moment later the place was jammed with men. Upstairs there were screams and a pistol shot. Trombo picked up Mike for fear of what Mike would do and carried him into the road.

The smoke was getting thicker until it was almost impossible to find anything but black in the sky. Red flames leaped high here and there to increase the terrible heat. Panting Spaniards fought among themselves over booty and, collecting it, threw it away and dashed on in the hope of better.

From another large house the steady bang of firing proceeded. Three groups of Spaniards had gathered there to storm the place, but they had little organization and rushed forward, only to stumble and fall grotesquely under the hammer of slugs from the roof of the flat-topped structure.

Now and then a gay headsilk was seen to ripple up there and perhaps eight or nine buccaneers were making a last stand of it.

The heap of bodies around the place grew slowly and then from the beach came fully thirty gunners with a cannon at the end of ropes. They swivelled the weapon around and crammed its mouth with round shot. It roared and bucked and a hole was in the wall. The sharpshooters on the roof got the gunner and then his successor. The men changed the angle of sight and poured a bucketful of musket balls into the smoking muzzle. Chips and splinters flew from the raised edge about the roof. The next load was round again and another section of the wall was smashed in. With a cheer the sailors and marines poured through the breach and swarmed up to the roof, though several were dropped down the stairs with shots from above, impeding the progress of the rest.

Trombo gave Mike another drink of brandy and Mike sat in the shade, looking somberly at the futile action in the house.

Screams and curses sounded on the roof amid the clang of steel on steel, and shortly, down came the successful stormers, lugging a few guns which they threw away in the street. One of them was buckling on a sword belt, but decided he didn't like it and cast it aside. Nine Spaniards were employed in a quarrel over booty which Mike could not see. They came closer to the doorway, hauling something.

Mike suddenly leaped into the house and snatched the pistols from his sash. They were dragging a woman with them and still fighting to get a cutlass away from her. Her face was bruised and darkened with powder grime. Her dress of fine silk was ripped from shoulder to waist. And even now she got free and cut at one of them. They bore her down to the floor and by stamping on her fingers got the cutlass away from her. Trombo had been much amused until he saw the expression on his almirante's face as Mike stalked forward.

"Almirante!" cried Trombo in fear. "They are too mad to know you! They will kill you!"

But Mike was deaf, for the woman beneath those battle stains was the Lady Marion!

At point-blank he let a sergeant have a ball in the stomach and a sailor the other in the face. And then his rapier was out and shimmering greedily.

"Let her go, you illegitimate sons," snarled Mike.

They leered drunkenly at him and recognized him not at all, for he, too, was blackened and his lace was torn. They let go the Lady Marion and sought to bring up weapons against him. The rapier licked the life from two as swiftly as two seconds fled and then Mike was smothered in their rush.

A mighty roar was above the pile and men were yanked away to have their heads bashed in against the walls. Shortly Trombo had the last one at squirming arm's length while Mike retrieved his sword and staggered forward towards the Lady Marion. This was the only egress from this room and so, trapped, armed again with a cutlass, she waited for him.

"Miguel Saint Raoul de Lobo," said Mike, bitterly. "Admiral of this rabble. Your arm, milady, so that I can escort you to the safety of my flagship."

She started to object and then understood the folly of staying here. She straightened up and with a slight curtsy, took his arm.

---

119

# CHAPTER EIGHT

The fleet was afraid of Mike, but behind his back even the officers raised a knowing brow. Mike had changed these past few months and perhaps some of the steel of his character was truly entering into him, for he had punished the rape of Tortuga with such thoroughness and attention to detail that half the men bore the mark of the bastinado and the other half wore the scars of Mike's withering beration. All ships were on half rations, despite the gigantic mound of stores which had been carried away from Tortuga. Marines, staring court-martial in the teeth, stalked outside storerooms and by the water casks.

"Sire," said long-faced Fernando, "you breed mutiny. These crews live like rats and die like mice under fever. Was it so terrible that they loosed their passions upon the English and French? After all, sire, think upon what the English and French have done to us!"

"Wrath begets wrath," said Mike.

"But we are armed to meet it."

"The Spanish colonies are not. One by one they'll be sacked. We've given Bristol and his hellions the excuse they need to sweep the Spanish from the Main."

"We can destroy them."

"If three pirate vessels had run into Tortuga last week while this fleet was unmanned, we would have been sunk to a ship."

"But they did not," said Fernando, brightly.

"And now every criminal and thief in the jails of France and Spain will be launched into the Caribbean to singe the King of Spain's beard. You're a pack of fools, Fernando."

Fernando flinched, for he was too high-born to bear insult. "I repeat, sire, that you breed mutiny."

"Then, sir, I'll deal with the fleet as one deals with mutineers." He felt a shadow fall upon the room and looked up to see Father Mercy. "Who gives you permission to come in here?" demanded Mike.

Father Mercy bowed and smiled until it seemed his face would crack.

"Why so pleased?" demanded Mike.

"The English captives, my son, are all safe under hatch, waiting for the church in Nombre de Dios."

"And that tickles your fancy," said Mike. "They are my prisoners, padre."

"Would you profit at the hands of God?"

"No," said Mike, "but you would. I repeat that they are mine, to do with as I like. Forget them."

"For a price," said Father Mercy, rubbing his hands, which gave out the sound of sandpaper.

"You bargain with me now," said Mike.

"You have in your cabin, my son, a heretic of—ah—special interest to me. I will trade you your other prisoners for her."

Mike stood up, angry. "Listen, you stinking fraud, if you say one more word about captives or about Lady Marion, I'll—I'll have you torn over your own rack! Now out before I change my mind and drill you where you stand." He reached for a pistol and Father Mercy almost fell over himself getting out of there.

But Father Mercy had the temerity to thrust his scaly head back in and say, "Think upon it. Your prisoners and your commission for one silly English heretic. Is it a fair trade, my son?"

---

Mike threw the pistol at the face and it vanished.

Fernando was grave. "Almirante, there is something strange about you. That was a father of the church, and yet—Don't you know it is madness to try to oppose such as he?"

"I have a fleet and he has a rosary," said Mike. "I leave it to you to discover which one fires the heaviest broadside."

"I think," said Fernando, leaving, "that you'll discover that it's the rosary."

Mike slumped down in his chair and stared at the door, which was now closed. He could hear the hiss of water from the open stern ports of his cabin and the ornate lamp swung rhythmically to and fro from the beams. He sat there for quite a while and then, with a shrug, poured out a drink.

There was a footfall at his side and he saw Lady Marion there. She had repaired her gown and removed the stains and after much rest looked herself again.

"I could not help but hear," said Lady Marion. "I am causing you a great deal of trouble."

"They pillaged against my orders," said Mike. "I am either almirante or I am not."

"If I know aught of sailors, such treatment is liable to be fatal."

"You know buccaneers," said Mike. "These are soldiers and sailors of Spain, not gutter sweepings and criminals."

"You imply an insult, I think."

"Think as you please," said Mike.

"I do," said the Lady Marion. "I know quite well that all this punishment, for instance, is to impress me with your own haloed innocence in the matter. Perhaps you count on my taking back word to St. Kitts that you aren't the demon you are painted. Well, sir, I know you now."

"Know me, do you?" said Mike.

"For a very clever and forceful gentleman," said the Lady Marion, "whom, in other circumstances, I might come to admire, if not for his mercy, at least for his audacity."

"Your praise is somewhat cold," said Mike.

"Aye, perhaps it is. I owe you my life, you think, forgetting that your fleet put my life in jeopardy. You are clever, but not quite clever enough, sir."

"You are conceited," said Mike, "to believe that I attacked Tortuga because I had heard you had gone there. I had not heard anything of the sort. You were sent away from St. Kitts because your father expected an attack on that place. I attacked Tortuga for the same reason—and to destroy possible pirate vessels and to weaken the defense of St. Kitts."

Her face was crimson. "You imply, sir, that I think so well of myself that your desire of me could cause what you have done."

"That," said Mike, "is what I imply."

"The only answer you have, sir, to make that a lie is to send me by advice boat and have me set down on St. Kitts."

"And that," said Mike, "is something I will not do."

She smiled, again at ease. "And why not?"

"Because," said Mike, "as much as I detest blowing away your cloud of self-esteem, I must hold you only because you are hostage against the behavior of Tom Bristol."

She stood. "If you for a moment think that Bristol will be stayed by such a thin threat, you are mad. He knows better than to trust any Spaniard and would expect to find me dead, whether he behaved or not. No, milord, you won't stop Tom Bristol. And you'll not succeed against him when he comes!"

"You," said Mike, "are more a fool than I thought you at first. To deny that I love you is folly. To deny your beauty is foolishness. But your charm is quite safe in my care, milady, for I've no taste for playing the part of a bungling buccaneer."

She crimsoned again and turning, slammed her cabin door behind her.

A few seconds later Mike was again appalled at himself. Why had he talked that way? It would have been so simple to have smoothed it all out. What was wrong with him? Here he was divorcing himself from fleet and church and from this woman as well—

But his words could not be recalled. He—

His words. *His* words. HIS WORDS!

Suddenly he shook an angry fist in the direction of the sky. "Damn you, Horace Hackett! So I'm to wreck my fleet, am I? So I'm to fall in love like a puppy with this English girl, am I? I'm to bowl myself over by opposing the church and then I'm to be murdered by your bucko-boy Bristol. Well, to hell with you and your damned typewriter! You're going to get something more than you expected before this thing is done!"

It was an empty boast, and Hackett's attention was now elsewhere—that he knew.

But heavens! He couldn't just sit here and walk straight to his death!

Death was such a terribly permanent affair!

No typewriter whirred above Nombre de Dios now. The ever-blue sea, the ever-wandering women, the ever-working slaves in the dockyards went on in their unvarying functions. The fever took its victims and, still hungry, took more. The merchants assembled for the transshipment of bullion and jewels and, as ever, swiftly dispersed as soon as a fleet had sailed.

And Mike brooded in his great, shadowy house as the weeks went by. Events were happening elsewhere. Nombre de Dios was in a lull before the storm began to blast it. And if Mike knew the plots of Horace Hackett, the latter quarter of the book had been entered upon and the latter quarter of Horace Hackett's book always dealt strictly with the victor and his savage surge to final victory. Horace Hackett had abandoned Nombre de Dios as a Spanish scene. Mike knew that when next it came under the invisible spotlight of Horace's questionable genius it would be with an English attack. No more pulling of Mike's puppet strings. No more painting the villain. That was all done and the villain was strictly upon his own, awaiting, despite anything he could do, his "just deserts."

In a way Mike was thankful, for it meant freedom of motion and speech. He would not again find his own mind betrayed into stupid actions and stilted speeches. He had a huge fleet, he had the guns of the fort to protect it. Behind him lay the Isthmus and the countless ambuscades into which the buccaneers must fall before they could come up to final grips. And if Horace Hackett thought he was going to push Tom Bristol through to the defeat of the Spaniards, the recovery of Lady Marion and the death of one Mike de Wolf without terrific opposition, then Horace Hackett had better go buy a plot jinni.

Left alone, Mike felt better. While it had been fine winning sword fights and forts with the help of the author, it had so irked Mike's sense of individuality that it was now almost with relief that he faced the final scenes, strictly on his own.

He could say what he wanted and do what he wanted.

Knowing Hackett, he knew this. That he could run away from the scene and responsibility had several times occurred to him, but he did not trust his apparent ability to escape. He had a feeling that if he sailed out it would be to captivity in the hands of the buccaneers. And if he ran away into the Isthmus either Father Mercy or the Indians would attend to his finish. No, he had to remain at his post and ready himself for the final onslaught.

He sent out pinnaces to flit up and down the coast with orders to scud back to Nombre de Dios with any intelligence of the English. He sent letters to the governors of other Spanish colonies advising them that the English would soon retaliate. He inspected his fleet, or some portion of it, almost daily and held many conferences with his captains.

But all was not well. That speech he had made to Father Mercy had undermined his influence. The near-mutiny which Horace—he now realized—had made him talk himself into was still in the atmosphere, making it even more sultry.

As Mike came up the walk to his house one afternoon he found Fernando waiting for him. The captain was spurred and mud-spattered after a hard ride from Panama across the mountains. His long face was haggard.

"*Buenas*," said Mike.

Fernando bowed, a little stiffly. "I come to seek you, sire, with dispatches from the governor at Panama."

Mike tossed his hat to a chair and let Trombo pull off the cloak.

He took the packet. "Well? You can tell me what's in them as well as though you'd read them."

Fernando crimsoned. "Yes, sire. The letter on top informs you that the panic you are spreading because of the English must be stopped because our blow at Tortuga will settle them for years to come. The next letter is from the bishop of Panama, telling you that you are to turn over the Lady Marion to Father Mercy for escort to Panama and examination by the bishop himself. The letter under that is from Anne, telling you that if you show so much preference for the English she will demonstrate the power of influence she has with the governor of Panama and that unless you give your Lady Marion over to the bishop, you may regret it. Forgive me for knowing these things but all Panama is sizzling with gossip about it."

"And you," said Mike, "let them sizzle."

Fernando shrugged.

"Perhaps you agree with them," said Mike.

Again Fernando shrugged. "Sire, I have already tried to make you understand the gravity of your action."

"Perhaps," said Mike, "you went to Panama just to make me see it further."

Fernando avoided his eyes.

"And perhaps," said Mike, "you'd like to have me show the white feather to Bristol by sending this woman back to him. If I did that, the English would have no high opinion of our ability to defend ourselves. It would be a tacit surrender. If I give over the Lady Marion to the bishop or Father Mercy, the results would be so horrible that no power on earth could stop this Bristol in his vengeance."

"And if you hold her here," said Fernando, "you destroy your own authority, your own career."

"Because of the stupidity of fools like you," said Mike, beginning to get mad. "Come into the house and ask the Lady Marion, if you like, what treatment she has received at my hands. Yes, of course, that shocks you. But come anyway."

And he forced Fernando inside.

The great hall stretched its shadowy depths before them for the blinds were drawn against the heat of the day. Massive furniture gleamed dully and the breeze rippled the tapestries.

"Trombo," said Mike, "inform the Lady Marion that we would like to see her here."

Trombo, like some hulking, hairless bear, waddled away. In the distance sounded a slammed door and a heavy thud and then Trombo came back feeling a new bruise upon his arm, looking guiltily at Mike. "She say 'no'."

Mike turned to Fernando. "She is my prisoner and nothing more. Now do you understand my position?"

Fernando looked at the bruise on Trombo's arm.

"Well—"

Mike took the packet of letters and tore them in half all at once. He handed the fragments, with seals intact, back to Fernando. "You had a hard ride, Captain. You've still a long way to go. Perhaps you had better be on your way."

"On my way? Whither?"

"To the governor of Panama, to the bishop, to Anne. Tell them what I have told you and give them back these. Tell them that they are the best allies that Tom Bristol ever had. Now go."

Fernando sighed and got up. He wanted badly to object for it is a long, long way from Nombre de Dios to Panama City and the Isthmus was acrawl with revolting Maroons. He tightened his sword belt and put on his cloak, and spurs rasping sullenly, went away.

"Trouble, my almirante?" said Trombo.

"Maybe."

"Almirante, I, Trombo, do not understand just how it is that this English woman can continue to disobey you. Why, no other woman ever hated the almirante. Maybe a good length of belt, neatly applied, might bring her—"

"I don't need your advice," said Mike. "Mutiny, religion, insubordination, and now you tell me how to handle women. Go take a jump in the first lake you meet!"

Trombo sorrowfully went away from there and left Mike to his woes. And for an hour or two Mike nursed them with feeling language. They were all so convinced of Spanish superiority!

All so sold on a man's duty to the church!

He paced back and forth, back and forth, passing each time a baby grand piano in the corner, reading, despite himself, the gold letters on it: Steinway, Chicago.

What a fraud all this was! What a mixed-up mess! He'd seen "Pittsburgh" on the steel cutlasses of the buccaneers and "C.I.O." stamped upon the lumber which was going into those galleons. Damn Horace Hackett for a blundering fool, unable to visualize a period completely. Why, it wouldn't be surprising to see Bristol hove into sight firing Lewis machine guns! Oh! By all that was unholy, why hadn't he (Mike) ever paid any attention to such crafts! Lewis machine guns against Bristol! But he knew he couldn't even fire one, much less make one. No amount of knowledge of a true world could correct anything in this.

To hell with that damned piano! And he banged both hands down on the keys. The instrument yelped in protest and Mike did it again. And then, because it was natural for him, he sank down on the bench and began to roll out a savage, melancholy concerto. But little by little the music soothed him and he began to play more softly.

For an hour and more his fingers roamed over the keys and he grew quieter until he had almost forgotten his troubles, aware only of music. It was with a start that he realized someone was standing against the window ledge looking at him. It was Lady Marion.

In her amber gown—for by author-magic she had landed here fully equipped—she looked even more heart-arresting than she had when he had seen her in St. Kitts.

"Don't stop," she said, quietly.

Mike did not stop but played on, softly, looking at her, wondering why she had been so violent to Trombo and himself before, but chose now to come out of her fortress. He guessed that she was about to plead for her own release and when that was refused, would begin to storm anew. But music evidently had its effect upon her and he was careful to maintain it.

"A little while ago," she said, "I saw one of your officers come here. With dispatches."

"Yes," said Mike, noncommittally.

"And when you sent for me and I refused to come—I opened the door again and heard what you said. In the many weeks—or is it months?—that I have been here I have learned some Spanish."

Mike cocked an ear at the ceiling and ceased playing for a moment.

No slightest sign of a typewriter. "Yes?" he urged, continuing his playing.

"You refused to turn me over to the church no matter how they threatened you. What would they do to me?"

"Burn you as a heretic."

"Yes—yes, I thought that was it."

"But you see no helmeted guard out there, with crosses on their chests, waiting, do you? You have nothing to fear."

"No—I don't think that I have. But I was not thinking of myself—so much. Your men think it strange that you keep me here. That Fernando has argued with you before to send me away."

"Yes. I refuse to pamper Bristol. And with you as hostage he might not attack."

"He won't believe you. He'll think me dead. You have a glib tongue, Michael; you proved that on St. Kitts. It would be much safer for you to send me away."

"So you ask for that again? Am I to trust the crew with which I would send you? Am I to risk a trap by trying to land you on St. Kitts?"

It occurred to Mike that instant that he was taking all this far too seriously and that, in addition, he was lying. He had moldered here for months, dreaming about her, thinking about her, aching for her, and now here she stood, the object of all that misery, the only true happiness for which he could hope before he perished, as perish he most certainly might at the hands of the soon-to-attack buccaneers.

His playing became dreamy. "You have a very bad opinion of me, milady, having seen me enact a rôle at St. Kitts to save my own neck and having witnessed the sack of Tortuga. And I have only to say that I did not order anything but a battle there, and am now in trouble because I punished my men so much for running amuck."

"I—realize that now."

"There is something which I have wanted to tell you for some time," continued Mike, looking only at the keys. "It has to do with why I am here, where I came from, where we are going." He lowered the music to somberness. "You do not know it, but you are only the character in a story. A lovely, devastating character, it is true, and one who is, I find, really alive." He waited for her to question that, but she was still.

"We," he continued, "are all characters in a story, nothing

more. But once I was in another world, the world which will some day read this story and be somewhat amused. There I know the author. And I know other stories by him and know how he thinks and writes so that here I also know. Bristol is going to storm this place. You will ultimately be returned to Bristol and I shall be killed. That is the way this story is scheduled to run. And I am trapped here. I came without being asked and was made to play this part of villain no matter how I opposed it. I am doubtful if I will ever return to that other world."

She was studying him. "Forsooth, sir, you carry that simile far. That playwright Shakespeare wrote in a play I saw in London that all the world is a stage and that we are merely the actors. But by what strange necromancy can you attempt the blasphemy of knowing God, knowing how He thinks and what He will do?"

"Your god, milady," said Mike, "is not the god you suppose him. You have lived your life in this world and this is only a world of fantasy. You remember far back and know that you were born, have people; you have seen pain and misery and happiness. You yourself are of warm, living flesh and blood. I give up the effort of trying to make you understand from whence I came and why I am here."

"No one ever asked to be born, few ever ask for the parts they have to play," said Lady Marion. "And all men, in all their actions, think they are doing exactly right. But, milord admiral, this is not settling the problem of my disposition."

"Yes," said Mike, "I think it is. Whatever I do and however I do it, the end will, of course, be the same. Bristol will win, will take you back and I will be killed."

"No one man can change destiny, milord, if you speak of that. I am afraid that it is only melancholy which leads you to such direful prophecy for yourself."

"You are here now," said Mike. "Why should I completely drown myself in misery by sending you away again? Let Bristol take you away—if he can. Let this plot run its course—if it will. But there is one thing, milady, which cannot change, and that—"

He stood up, facing her.

She looked up into his face with sudden awareness and her breathing quickened. Her hands were slightly raised as though to fend him off, but not so high as actually to do so. "Milord—" she said, tremulously.

"Milady," said Mike, gathering her to him and holding her tightly against him. "I love you," he whispered.

She thrust at him and tried to get free, but his arms were strong and his lips, seeking hers, were gentle. And then her arms ceased their flailing and her hands crept up across his flat, straight back and locked there. "Oh—my darling," she whispered.

# CHAPTER
# NINE

For a month direful news came to Nombre de Dios by a seemingly endless stream of messengers. The pirates had sacked Robelo. They had gutted a merchantman and put her crew to the plank. Bristol himself had led an attack upon Santa Ysabel and not a Spaniard in the fortress had been left alive. Everywhere the buccaneer fleet ranged in search of the Spanish fleet, but ships were slow and, at this season, winds were few. The advice boats and scouts of Miguel Saint Raoul de Lobo failed utterly to locate the elusive pinnaces and carracks under the bloody banner of England. Refugees—those few who got through the wilderness and past the Indians—came crawling into Nombre de Dios with tales of horror which set Spanish teeth on edge.

"You must attack! You must find them and wipe them from the seas!" howled Governor Bagatela, banging his cane down on the walk and turning purple.

"Aye, and leave this harbor with only your forts to hold it," said Mike. "To leave completely open the road to Panama. If I contact them for certain, I'll attack. But to wander out upon the Main with every Indian on the shore passing information on to the English, would be to do just what Bristol wants us to do. Here we stay until they are seen."

And Fernando, commanding a galleon out on scout, came back without word of the buccaneers save that he had found Terra Nueva a charred patch of black strewn with what bodies the Caribs had considered inedible.

"They've loosed the Indians upon us," said Fernando. "They've given them guns and knives and hatchets and it's said the English are paying a bounty of a pound for every Spanish head that is brought to them."

"That last is a lie," said Mike. "Bristol is in command of that fleet somewhere out there and Bristol only wants one thing. He probably seeks to draw us away from this place by attacking small, unfortified spots. Then, by a list of successes, he continually strengthens his fleet. Bristol wants the Lady Marion back, for he must know from spies here that she is still alive. His men want gold. They don't give a damn about king and empire. They're buccaneers, already scarred with the bastinadoes and cats of his majesty's royal navy. Calm down. Eventually Bristol will have to make his brag good and attack Nombre de Dios. When he does we'll roll him up like a sheet of paper and throw him away."

It was a definite stand to take, but he could take it with the powers he had. Messages from the governor of Panama he answered all in one phrase, "Are you so eager to be gobbled by the buccaneer that you'll remove me?" Sheer bravado, but it had a slight effect.

Father Mercy, white-hot for English blood, came storming to the house on the hill. "They're murdering priests! They're killing every Spaniard that wears the cross. They're exalting the blasphemous Protestant creed! Out after them, you coward! Why do you sit here shivering in port while they sweep Spain from the Main? Does that English—"

Mike struck him to his knees and Father Mercy, in real terror, his rage quite cooled, looked up at the tall, handsome devil whose rapier point licked avidly before the priestly nose.

"Down that hill and into your church," said Mike. "Pray for the souls of the people killed by the buccaneers and add a prayer for yourself, thanking your God that He put me in between the buccaneer fleet and the shore here at Nombre de Dios. They'll string you up fast enough as it is if they catch you."

Father Mercy went down the hill.

Another month passed with more alarms and wild guess-
es and sacked villages and vanished cargo vessels, and Mike
waited patiently, knowing very well that he could do no good
ranging the Main, and understanding clearly Bristol's real
goal. Bristol would have to come to Nombre de Dios.

A short message went out from Mike via an Indian who
was suspected of being a spy:

SIR PIRATE:

Your fate is already determined. I object seriously to being
considered so thick-witted as to mistake your true intentions.
Butchering Spaniards from Cartagena to Florida may keep
your men amused, but personally the uproar you've created
bores me. The Lady Marion is well and safe as the bearer, who
is probably in your pay, will attest. Kindly fall upon Nombre
de Dios so that we can have done with you.

Your obedient servant,

MIGUEL ST. R. DE LOBO
ALMIRANTE

P. S. The Lady Marion wishes to send her love.

The note was answered a few weeks later:

SIR SPY:

Please tell the Lady Marion that we are coming after her
immediately and please have her bags packed.

BRISTOL

"I hope," said Mike at the supper table that night, "that Bristol is as good a commander as he is made out to be. Or perhaps that the god in the case is witty enough to see the import behind this."

"You make me uncomfortable with your talk of 'god,' Mike."

The candlelight caught in her hair, flame answering flame. And the goblet of wine which she held matched her beautiful eyes. Mike grinned happily. Why shouldn't he be happy for a little while?

"Shall I order your bags packed, my dear?" said Mike.

"That little horse you gave me today is a darling," said the Lady Marion.

And so the matter stood.

Mike was not in error about Hackett this time, for such an obvious bit of strategy could not go past without notice. No admiral with any sense at all would hurl a fleet at a port which was expecting him. Rather he would hold off, prepare himself, lie quiet for a space and so convince the enemy that he does not wish to accept the challenge.

And so Mike won a little more time—which proved his own undoing.

# CHAPTER
# TEN

The gold train came from Panama. Little mules gay with bells, musketeers brave in yellow and scarlet and steel, merchants who had waddled over the rough trail in slave-borne sedan chairs, and gold, emeralds, silver and silver and emeralds and gold came streaming into Nombre de Dios. And with them came Lord Entristecer, governor of Panama.

Nombre de Dios glittered and hummed and the surface of the harbor was laced by the wakes of boats and barges dashing to and fro. The ships from Spain stood salt-stained in the roads awaiting their precious cargoes and the Spanish fleet swung dazzlingly from cables, looking dangerous. All day and all night the town teemed with people and resounded with music and quarreling.

The governor of Panama and the governor of Nombre de Dios—the latter being much junior—dined in state with all the nobles present. Great platters of meat and high bottles of wine and dishes of gold and a slave behind each chair. It was a gala dinner, entirely too gay to foreshadow disaster. And yet when it was done, Lord Entristecer withdrew into the coolness of the drawing room, indicating that he wanted only three men to accompany him—Lord Bagatela, Mike and Captain Fernando.

"Gentlemen," said the melancholy lord of the New World, "I have news."

"And I, also, have news," said Mike.

"Yours first, then," said the sad governor.

"It is probable that the fleet will be attacked on the high seas by Bristol and the English," said Mike, "for all this gold is high bait. It is my plan, which I may tell you in detail later, to send only a small escort with the plate fleet and to keep the main body to windward in such a way as to catch the English napping. For I've a notion that when Bristol sees how few are guarding the plate fleet he will detach but few to take it. Then Bristol will send the bulk of his ships to attack Nombre de Dios. Up will come our fleet, crush the portion of Bristol's and then, turning, come down on Nombre de Dios and crush him against the guns of the forts. This plan is based on my knowledge of the psychology of—of Bristol. If—"

"Your news is not news," said the melancholy old man from Panama. "It is strategy which looks very slim. And, Sir Miguel, it is not likely to be put to use."

"How's this?" said Mike. "Am I not admiral of—"

"You are not," said the governor from Panama. "Today, with the coming of the ships from Spain, I received this dispatch from his most Catholic majesty the king." He took it out and unrolled it. "As you can see for yourself, Sir Miguel, it removes you from command. I had asked for more, but this is all the reply. You will notice that it places Captain Fernando in complete charge of naval operations on the Main."

Mike steadied himself and gave Fernando a contemptuous glare and then, before they could say more, he stalked from the room.

Much later that night, sitting in the moonlit window of his room, Mike imparted the news to the Lady Marion.

"Then—then," she said, "you no longer can command anything?"

"Neither afloat nor ashore," said Mike.

"Who did this?"

"Several people."

"And I—I have been the cause of it all!"

"No," lied Mike. "Oh, no!"

"Oh, yes," she wept.

"Have you no thought of what might happen to you?" said Mike.

Evidently she had not yet considered that, but she looked up at him proudly.

"You would not let them touch me."

"No," said Mike. "No, of course not."

And in the morning, when Father Mercy came armed with stacks of documents and accompanied by two squads of church troops, he found the entrance to the admiral's home barricaded.

"Open up!" cried Father Mercy. "Open up in the name of God!"

A bullet clipped the hairs of his head and he hastily went down the hill again, his soldiers tumbling after.

Five days later a ship stood into the roadstead of Nombre de Dios. She moved sluggishly for her belly was full of sea water and her masts had been mowed as though by a scythe. But, limping under jury rig, wanly flying her battle flag from a splintered truck, she managed to brace about for the last mile up the channel and get her anchor down.

There was something sorrowful about the way she swung into the wind.

The town went down to cluster on the quay and wait silently for news.

A barge went out, carrying Lord Bagatela.

"Make way," whispered the people in the back of the crowd. And people moved to one side and the tall, ominous figure of Mike made its way to the stone steps where the barge must land upon its return.

A priest squeaked in excitement and dashed off to find some church troops, but Mike did not even deign to notice his going. Hand on hilt, cloak stirring a little in the wind, he waited for the slowly rowed barge.

When Lord Bagatela came alongside the quay his face was chalky. And in the cockpit beside him lay a blanched gentleman in blood-soaked silk who already had the grey of death upon his aristocratic face. Captain Fernando was handed up. He saw Mike standing there and reached out feebly and pleadingly towards him.

"Almirante," whispered Fernando. "They . . . attacked in full force . . . thousands of them. Only . . . only my flagship got away. . . after it could do nothing more. Of the fleet . . . there are not thirty men left alive, for there was no quarter. It's . . . all gone . . . Almirante. Your fleet . . . I should never have helped take it from you. I want to be forgiven . . . please, Almirante. I am dying."

"Aye," said Mike, sadly. "You're forgiven. May whatever__ place you go to have a kinder god than this. Good luck, Fernando."

Mike turned aside as they bore the captain away. No typewriter in the sky here. Nothing but real, agonizing death. Those streaks down from the scuppers of the *Josef y Maria*, real blood had made those.

"There he is!" cried a priest, excitedly. "There he is!" And some thirty church troops rushed in to close on Mike—and found Lord Bagatela between their quarry and themselves.

"Stay!" cried Bagatela. "Stay, or my guard will fire!" And his guard leaped to man the bow chaser of the small barge.

"He's an infidel!" cried Father Mercy. "He disobeys the church!"

"You've no authority to touch one of my staff, church or no church!" roared Bagatela.

"He is not one of your staff!" howled Father Mercy.

"If he had commanded that fleet, the buccaneers would be dead to a man!" countered Bagatela. "I see it now. He had a plan and that plan would have worked. And now, just when we may be attacked, you wish to throw him on a rack. Think of your own filthy necks, you hell-hounds!"

Father Mercy stopped, for the populace was beginning to take it up and it is never good policy for a member of the church to show such thirst for vengeance against such protest.

Father Mercy and the other priests backed up and with them went their troops. And Mike forgot about them. He was already looking to the sea.

"How's that, eh?" said Lord Bagatela. "How's that?"

"Thanks," said Mike, indifferently. "Do you think your forts can withstand a bombardment from a fleet?"

"Maybe," said Bagatela. "But a fleet that size, such as Fernando reported—"

"I'm thinking so myself. Governor, have the guns off the *Josef y Maria*, for she's no use to us now. Have them mounted here on the shore to oppose landing. If they get past your forts, they'll try to sweep ashore and we'll meet them here with grape."

"You have authority," said Bagatela, eagerly, sweating at the picture Mike had so indifferently painted. "Do anything you like, sir. Anything!"

"It will be little enough now," said Mike. "Oh, well—get a runner off to Panama City. If we fall here, they'll come across the Isthmus and attack there. Get reinforcements if you can, but I don't think we'll have time before the devils stop binding up their wounds."

"Immediately," said Bagatela, hurrying off.

Mike smiled a little. It had its points, this business of being branded, so offhandedly, a military genius and by that token alone becoming one. Well! There was little hope now, but he'd try what he could. In one respect he *had* changed the plot and so he had a very faint hope that he might change it further.

With fury, then, he went about the task of trying to make that faint hope bloom.

"And so," said Horace Hackett, grandly laying aside his latest chapter, "that is how it goes to date. Now Bristol—"

Jules shook his head sorrowfully. "I don't like it."

Horace looked around the chromium-plated office as though searching for a witness to this blasphemy. He found one in René LaFayette, who, manuscripts on his lap, was dozing comfortably awaiting his turn with the publisher.

"You hear that?" said Horace. "You hear that, René? He says he doesn't like it. He says he doesn't like the greatest sea battle ever written!"

"I didn't, either," said René, helpfully.

"See?" said Jules. "He didn't, either. And from the way you are protesting I think you don't like it either, Horace."

"Me? Why I sweat blood writing that sea fight! Can't you just see Bristol, swooping at the head of his hellish crew down upon the Spaniards? Can't you hear the roar of cannon and the screams of maimed and mangled men? Can't—"

"Nope," said Jules, "and you can't, either." He looked accusingly at Horace. "That's what you writers always do. You take some point in your yarn that you don't like and so you figure an editor won't like it, so you come in and tell the editor just how swell that point is. You writers are a lot of fakes!"

Mortally wounded, judging from the appearance of his round, somewhat oily face, Horace sank back and was silent.

"Nope," said Jules, "I don't like it. Where was this Spanish admiral, huh? You don't say a word about this Spanish admiral in this whole fight. Bristol comes up and there's the Spanish fleet. So Bristol tackles them and the Spanish fleet sinks. That ain't tough enough, see? You got to have it a lot tougher on Bristol. Now what's he got to fight but a few shore batteries? And do you think them Spaniards would be so stupid as to send out a lot of gold when there was a pirate fleet waiting to take it? And—"

"All right," said Horace, peeved. "All right, I didn't think it was so good, either."

"Well, your strong man in this story is this Spanish admiral and where was he?"

"I dunno," said Horace. "You got to understand that sometimes, when you're writing, a story just takes care of itself."

"Well, that one didn't. Here you are at the climax, and yet you ain't got any Spanish admiral in charge of that fleet or anything. This is a sea story, not a land story, and if Bristol is going to get this Spanish admiral to rights and recover Lady Marion, why, it's got to be done on the sea. They gotta have a fight on the quarterdeck of the admiral's flagship."

"That's been done!" said Horace.

"So what? It was good, wasn't it?" Jules, having won his point, looked smug. "Now you get up a fight that won't look like two kids swatting at each other with straws. This has got to be powerful, see? It's the whole story!"

"You mean I've got to tear up perfectly good copy?" said Horace.

"Why not?" said Jules, unsympathetically. "It ain't good anyway."

"You hear that, René? He says to tear up pages and pages!"

"You're lucky he didn't make you tear up the book if it's all as lousy as that," said René.

"Nuts," said Horace. "Just because a guy can write good you expect him to write good all the time! All right, I'll tear up that chapter and to hell with your deadline."

"You tear it up *and* rewrite it *and* get it in here in time to go to press Monday or I'll—I'll let Tritewell illustrate it!"

Horace shuddered. "All right," he surrendered. He got up and gathered the manuscript into its envelope and slouched away. When he passed René LaFayette he muttered, "And after all the drinks I've bought *you.*"

René grinned.

# CHAPTER
# ELEVEN

A ll was serene in the town of Nombre de Dios. The monotonously blue sea spread without a ripple beyond the channel and the empty bay was undisturbed save for two barges hauling cannon out of the wreck of the *Josef y Maria*.

The shore battery, protected by logs and screened by brush behind the quay, was growing with the sweat of several hundred Indian slaves. Up and down through the works strode Mike, making suggestions, ordering changes, attending to the best disposition of the guns. He was weighed upon by the impossibility of holding this place against such a fleet as he knew was coming.

Now and again before, sudden reinforcements of one character or another had magically appeared, but so far, nothing untoward had happened. And for three toilsome days he had flayed this battery into existence, working three shifts through the hot days and nights until he himself was worn to gauntness. In addition he had sent out small vessels with orders to return instantly with any word of the buccaneers, and these reports awakened him each time he tried to rest.

The Lady Marion had been very sweet, but she had not mentioned that he should rest for fear he might take this adversely, believing her still anxious to be rescued—which she most certainly was not, even to the point of writing a note to Bristol and sending it by a known spy.

At three o'clock that afternoon, Lord Bagatela came waddling down to see what went on and within another half-hour Mike had laid his last gun.

Mike, mopping at his face with a linen kerchief given him by Trombo, paused to wave it in the direction of the long battery.

"Well, there she is," said Mike. "And now we'll have up the powder and balls and grape and we can at least make it uncomfortable for them when they arrive."

"Uncomfortable?" gaped Bagatela. "My dear Almirante, I do hope that you can promise more than that!"

"I'm too tired to be optimistic," said Mike.

Bagatela looked along the battery and sighed. "I do hope something comes of this. You've worked these men to rags and when I think of that, it reminds me that you haven't slept a great deal, either. Shouldn't you take a rest after all this labor? So that your thoughts will be clear if they come on the morrow?"

"I suppose I should," said Mike. "Well, I'll be off. If anything happens, call me immediately."

"Indeed, I will!" said Bagatela.

Mike started up the curving road through the town towards his house. And then it happened!

There was ripping sound somewhere high overhead. The whole coast trembled! There was a repetition of splashes in the harbor and a shaking roar along the beach! All went dark!

Mike was no longer on the path; he was on the quarter-deck of the *Josef y Maria*!

Dazedly he gazed around him through the night, surprised that all was so calm again and that the few sailors who worked as a deadeye did not seem aware of anything having taken place. There was a full moon in the sky and, if Mike remembered properly, "last night" had seen the moon in its last quarter. By the brilliance of it he had a clear view of the beach and another shock.

No shore battery!

Days and days of work and now no sign!

Anxiously he scanned the forts which before had been wholly on the north side of the channel. Now there were not only twice as many ramparts and embrasures on the north side, but also a massive fortress directly across from it on the south side!

The character of the town seemed but slightly altered save that it was bigger, better lighted and appeared to have more people in it, judging from the amount of music and laughter which came out across the water.

Mike took a turn around the deck. He was not even jolted to find the harbor filled with ships. Yes, filled. Nearly the entire Spanish naval fleet as well as the plate ships were there in force, lighted like churches and just as rugged.

"Almirante!"

Mike turned to find Captain Fernando, in the best of health, at his side.

"Almirante, I have just received word from an advice-boat captain that the buccaneer fleet is now but a few leagues from Nombre de Dios and coming up a strong wind astern!"

Mike heard Fernando and he also heard something else— the faint rattle of keys high in the sky.

"Very good," Mike heard himself say. "You may fire recall guns and have trumpeters sound quarters. How much does it lack until dawn?"

"Five hours, Almirante."

"Aye, five hours. And within seven those English dogs will be shark bait. Pass the word for a captains' conference."

"Aye, aye, sir," said Fernando.

When Fernando had gone away an ominous grey shape drifted across the quarterdeck towards Mike. "Almirante," simpered Father Mercy, "I would like now to make claim for the English captives. The rack starves for heretics."

Mike was about to make violent retort when from his lips came the words "Aye, the rack must be fed and the stake as well. You'll have fodder for your religious zeal before the night and day are done, Father Mercy."

"Thank you, Almirante. And the fellow Bristol?"

"Ah, Bristol," Mike heard himself say. "Father, if there's anything left of Bristol, ye're welcome."

"The English girl," said Father Mercy. "What about her now?"

"The Lady Marion," said Mike, angry at being a puppet but helpless, "is my particular own—if I can tame her."

Father Mercy grinned evilly and drifted away.

While trumpets blared and drums rolled and recall cannon thundered, Mike leaned on the taffrail of the *Josef y Maria* and looked on. Barges came flying back to the ships a-glitter with the helms, corselets and pikes of the soldiery. The vessels teemed with confident activity and orders flew swiftly back and forth.

And then the typewriter in the sky faded away and left the activity continuing.

Mike was worried. Quarter moons which became full moons instantly and a fleet which sprang back up out of Davy Jones's locker and dead men walking again were no worry to him. But those words he had said about the Lady Marion, about the English captives—Things had changed. And Marion—

He leaped down to the waist from the sterncastle and bawled for his barge. When it was laid alongside the stage he jumped into the stern sheets and gripped the tiller. Trombo dropped into the bow and Trombo's bastinado cracked out to give energy to the oarsmen.

The barge fairly leaped through the water under Mike's urging and swerved in alongside the quay. With the command to wait, Mike sprang to the dock and started up the hill towards his house. But Lord Bagatela was there to make him pause.

"All is ready ashore, Almirante. Your trap is laid for them and we cannot help but win. How goes the sea?"

"All's well," said Mike. And edging away, "Did you notice anything strange a while ago?"

"Strange?" said Bagatela. "No, can't say that I did."

"And the full moon?" said Mike. "It was at its last quarter last night."

"Oh, I've seen those things happen before," said Bagatela. "The will of God."

"And the fleet out there?" said Mike. "It's there again."

"Why, it's been there all along, hasn't it? Why? What should have happened to it?"

Mike departed, fearing the worst. He was greeted with huzzahs as he hastened through the streets and several times had to refuse to stop and drink to victory.

On the veranda of his house he paused, wondering if he could take what was coming and he knew now that come it must. A servant threw open the door for him and he strode in.

"The Lady Marion?"

"Is in her room, under guard as usual," said the servant.

Mike motioned away the guards and thrust open her door. He stopped.

Tall and regal, her face wreathed with disdain, she faced him. "Well, now, Sir Admiral! You did not expect Bristol to come, and yet come he has! And he'll pick your rotten bones before night."

"Aye, so even you think he's a vulture!" said Mike. He had tried to stop that, but now again he was aware of the clicking sound on high.

"Now go to your defeat!" said the Lady Marion. "My curse shall follow you!"

Mike got mad. Unaccountably mad. He slammed the door and rushed away, down the hill towards his ships and as he went, to the sound of bugles blaring, the clicking again faded. Mike ceased to be angry and was only hurt. He stopped and faced about, irresolute.

Marion! His darling Marion! Marion, whose sweet head upon his shoulder had solaced these long months of waiting, whose lips had drawn away the bitterness of his being trapped. And now—

There was no use. Desolated, he went on down the hill. Bristol. All this had to be fixed for Bristol! Bristol, a damned puppet!

Well, he'd see about that. He had a huge fleet and the harbor was now so strong that anything short of a miracle would find it staunch. He must not allow himself to be betrayed now. He'd do for Bristol and then, coming back, he'd awaken the love which Marion had had for him.

"Damn you!" said Mike, shaking his fist at the sky. "I'll show you! Do you hear me? I'll knock your fair-haired son of a witch into the briny and then we'll see what you'll do about it! I'm going to *win!*"

And back aboard the *Josef y Maria* he stalked up and down the table, past the swinging lanthorns, past the eager faces of his captains, and gave them their orders.

"Guerrero," said Mike. "Your squadron will act as a decoy. You will draw away from the battle line as though fleeing and when the pirate comes through that hole you will about ship and knife his column in two. Then you, Bolando, with your three vessels, will come up into the action and crush Bristol's spearhead against our battle line's rear. And you, Sorenzo, will swing your squadron on our left wing in a half-moon so as to engulf the half of Bristol's fleet which will not pass through the break. We will then maneuver to do all possible damage and finally, draw off to seaward. The wind will force Bristol down upon the forts and while we hold off on a broad reach, both our vessels and the forts will hammer him to fragments. Above all things, gentlemen, watch the flagship for your signals. And do not allow yourself to be boarded, for the soul of this strategy is to split up Bristol, wreak havoc to his ships and then throw him into a position where destruction to his fleet is inevitable. That is all. We sail in a half hour. His most Catholic majesty expects every man to die rather than surrender."

Glowing with confidence the captains trooped out. And Mike stared after them until they had gone, still resolute.

# CHAPTER
# TWELVE

Dawn cracked like the firing of a pistol and there was the sun, just up over the eastern horizon, a great scarlet ball which sent ribbons of flame quivering across the zenith. The sea was smooth and though this hour in these waters should have had no wind, there was wind, about twenty miles of it, quite sufficient to send prows knifing and foaming. But no ships were moving.

In this moment all was still. There was the buccaneer fleet, a long line of small, fast vessels drawn in battle order from north to south. Here was the Spanish fleet, huge and ponderous and brilliantly gilded, drawn in a parallel line. There was a mile and a half of open water between them and the black silhouettes of the English against the sun.

Mike, cloaked against the dawn chill, leaned his telescope against the deckhouse to steady it and focused it upon the English fleet but he could see nothing, for he was nearly blinded by the sun.

He lowered the brass and shook his head.

As nearly as he could tell, they had two-to-one superiority over these English, broadside for broadside, but Mike was no longer a trusting sort. The lead ship opposite his own he supposed to be Bristol's, for it resembled the *Fleetfoot*, the vessel he, Mike, had stolen from St. Kitts. Just how it had got back into Bristol's command he was not sure, but there it was. Behind the *Fleetfoot* ranged thirty-six vessels of varying sizes, but all rigged square without a lateen showing on any stick.

The ships were sailing now and water hissed under the stern of the *Josef y Maria* while braces creaked in the strain of swift air, driving the vessel harder. Behind her plowed nearly fifty Spanish ships of line. This heartened Mike in one respect, but in another made him nervous, for he had left port with but twenty. A rake of his telescope showed him that all bore the ensign of the Caribbean command and so were his vessels, and that the men on their decks were numerously standing to quarters with linstocks lighted. Marines were in their tops, matches poised until they came within musket distance. Gun captains checked the lay of their pieces and all went on in a quite usual manner.

The two battle lines were forging towards a point where they would range.

"Fire me a serpentine, extreme range," said Mike to Fernando. "We'll gauge by it."

The word was passed and a serpentine crew on the main deck elevated the weapon's muzzle with handspikes and slid quoins out until the base of the cannon was resting on the last bed of the carriage.

"Clear!" said the gun captain.

The gunners leaped aside and put a strain on the breechings which limited the recoil. The gun captain ran a line of powder with his belt horn down from the touchhole, along the gun to the base ring. He smartly applied his smoking linstock, snapping his hand out of the way. There was a huff and a spit and a thin line of hot smoke soared from the touchhole.

*Bam!*

The cannon leaped upwards about three feet and back about six, the crew straining at the breechings. The white smoke engulfed the port and the side of the ship and the crew.

The fifty-three-and-a-half-pound ball skittered over the sea and plunkered into a swell two thousand paces from the ship, about five hundred short of the closing *Fleetfoot.*

"Toss a basilisk into him just to show him we can," said Mike.

The word was passed forward to the fo'c'sle where the long-range five-inch cannon usually acted as bow chasers. The crew there slewed the short carriage about, blocking the wheels against the roll. Ten pounds of powder in a parchment cartridge went down the muzzle, followed by the wadding and the fifteen-pound shot. The muzzle was elevated and the gun captain applied his powder horn and then cried, "Clear!" The linstock drew a huff of flame.

*Bam!*

Mike lost track of the ball against the sun, but in a moment saw a spar come tumbling down from the *Fleetfoot*'s foremast.

"All basilisks," said Mike. "At will."

Pennons went rushing up the signal hoist and a moment later the Spanish fleet had its light long-rangers in action.

The English could not yet reply to this sparse fire. Up and down the Spanish battle line at long intervals, puffs of smoke and thunder indicated the loss of more English rigging.

"We're closing in," said Mike. "Stand ready with cannon royal on the gun deck."

The signal hoist was alive again and word went down to fifty gun decks. Battery captains poised themselves at the forward end of their long batteries and waited. Gun captains waited on the battery captains.

The range narrowed down to eighteen hundred paces.

"Fire!" said Mike.

On fifty ships battery captains loped from fore bulkhead to aft, chopping down a hand as each gun was passed. If they had all been fired at once, the gunwales would not have stood the strain. And so their flame and fury lasted down the length of the vessel for half a minute, lasting over the fleet for nearly three minutes and hiding all the gilt and all the flags completely in a fog.

"Wear ship," said Mike.

The signal could not be seen, but it was a usual maneuver. Presenting a stern to the enemy while smoke hid much of the vessel, the ship of line could go downwind as it turned, thus staying with the smoke a little longer and coming out of it with the fully loaded banks bearing.

"Fire," said Mike.

Thunder again engulfed the Spanish fleet and once more the water and air, bulkheads and spars around the English received a murderous drubbing. While only twenty percent of the broadsides began to take any effect, there was weight enough in those sixty-six-pound cannon royals to blast the heart out of any enemy.

Again and again the maneuver was repeated, perfectly timed, the loading going on with haste while the loaded batteries were presented and fired. But now the English with their demi-cannon were getting to work. The third-of-a-hundredweight balls plunked noisily into the sea and sprayed the decks, plucked spars down and knocked great gouges in the bulkheads, sending violent and jagged splinters flying everywhere, deadlier than shrapnel.

The guns were getting hot and had to be swabbed, which slowed the Spanish firing. Now, when they recoiled, they very often leaped violently to crash against the beams overhead or knocked themselves on their sides or, getting free, wiped out their gun crews in a breath and went thundering on across the gun decks to batter havoc everywhere until at last caught and overturned.

Mike paced back and forth, splinters plucking at him, feeling the acrid powder smoke in his lungs, already deaf from the cannonading and almost blind. The sun, though the engagement had already lasted an hour, was not one inch higher above the horizon than it had been at the beginning!

Until now Mike had taken this thing as a matter of course, for there lurked in his mind a carelessness born of the fact he was a puppet and that all this was stage scenery. But now happened a thing which hurled him into reality with soul-shocking force.

The buccaneer fleet had worked in to within six hundred paces, pouring in a continuous cannonade and taking fearsome punishment. And now, by double-charging their few mammoth cannon royal and shooting them with chain-connected balls, they commenced upon the clear of the galleon quarterdecks and the severance of shrouds. One such shot came tumbling like a loose dumbbell from the *Fleetfoot*, swinging round and round, travelling slowly enough to be visible. It swung ponderously one last time as it passed over the quarterdeck of the *Josef y Maria*. Captain Fernando did not even give it pause, for it mangled him into two chunks and his feet still stepped back to brace as shoulders and head were squashed against the helm, spattering the quartermasters.

Mike had flinched and now, staring, he felt himself turn green-white. From there his glance, shocked to acuteness, swept to the waist of the vessel and saw how red the scuppers ran into the sea, how the sand laid down to prevent slipperiness from just this cause had been washed away. Tangles of spars and lines, splinters, the smoking ruins of cannon, the smashed gunwales, the heaps of slain from which came tributaries to feed the scuppers' flowing, made him shiver. Above the ceaseless roar of guns and the shrill cracking of musketry sounded the agonized screams of the wounded and dying.

He fought to get back his hold on his nerves, to cultivate again that contemptuous air of detachment, to remind himself that all this was in the hands of one Horace Hackett. He regained his nerve in a few moments, but not for any of these reasons.

It was Bristol who was doing this to him, Bristol who would soon defeat him, Bristol who would soon take back forever the woman Mike loved.

Angry now, Mike commanded the hoist once more and up leaped the gay flags from out of the white smoke and into the sunlit sky beside the topmasts.

Whether the order was obeyed or not, Mike could not tell. But within a very few minutes the line of English ships bent in the centre, making a V which speared into the break and must have appeared at the far end of the Spanish battle line.

Mike cupped his hands and bawled the order to his sailing-master which sent the wounded *Josef y Maria* about on a tack to beat eastward across the stern of the *Fleetfoot*, thus crossing the English T. The plainly done sterncastle of the buccaneer vessel loomed through the choking mist, prey to the higher guns of the great galleon.

With the chop of his hand Mike sent his battery captains rushing aft, causing each cannon of the starboard broadside to batter murderously into the *Fleetfoot*. Balls from snipers in the buccaneer's rigging tore up wood about Mike's feet as the stern of the *Fleetfoot* came abeam and then abaft of the *Josef y Maria*. Not a port light or a plank was left in the *Fleetfoot*'s stern and so close had been the gun mouths that fire now jabbed greedily among the ruin. Fore and aft the *Fleetfoot*'s decks had been swept by splinter and ball and now her main began to tilt slowly to starboard while the topmen either dived widely into the sea or sought to scramble down. The *Fleetfoot* was a shuddering ruin.

The ship next in line behind Mike took the buccaneer next to the *Fleetfoot*, passing between it and the wreck and blowing it, like its mate, into fragments. No. 3 Spanish ship crossed the T the third English ship down, and again made a quivering horror out of a once-saucy bark. No. 4 Spanish took No. 4 English again, and so went the succession of penetrations, like a multi-fingered hand penetrating the gaps of its multi-fingered mate.

That the English were still able to move at all was a shock to Mike, for when he looked back he saw that the *Fleetfoot*, splinters, corpses and flames, still proceeded towards the break in the Spanish line, even though the *Josef y Maria*'s sister, which had been at the other end, had begun the same awful toll of that side of the English V. And, even though the squadron which had pulled out to make the trap came about, cutting through the English, that still did not stop the infiltration of the buccaneers through the Spanish formation.

Punished until it was incredible that it could still float, the buccaneer fleet finally gained the leeward of the Spanish fleet and went coursing down towards Nombre de Dios.

Mike made a hasty survey of his vessels. Fully twenty were in sinking condition, their crews fighting off sharks in the water, the screams of the wounded cut off and turned on gruesomely by the slap of the waves. With signals, Mike caused several of the Spanish vessels to swerve out of line to pick up survivors and then, with the *Josef y Maria* making the final cut of the figure-eight maneuver which his fleet had executed so to rake the buccaneers, steered for the stragglers of the buccaneers and began to chop them to chunks with calculatingly murderous fire as he passed them close aboard.

There was elation struggling to surge up from Mike's heart, but he kept it down until this was done. Now he would ride the English up against the channel batteries at Nombre de Dios, and if a man escaped it would be only because the Spanish had willed to pick him up as a prisoner. And the buccaneers seemed unaware of the two-sided press which was about to crush them. This and this alone worried Mike now. It did not seem possible that Bristol, the vaunted Captain Bristol, could so foolishly allow himself to be smashed in such a trap.

Still—there were the buccaneers, sailing handsomely, even eagerly, into the jaws of destruction.

Mike paced the quarterdeck. Now and again, as the *Josef y Maria* turned to cross a wounded English quarter and blast him completely out of action, he looked uneasily along the wrecked decks for Bristol. That he had not seen Bristol when the *Fleetfoot* had been raked worried him. That he was succeeding worried him. That he had not heard any clattering on high worried him further still.

There was decidedly something very spooky about this action. He was winning it!

Behind him the sun still hung its inches above the horizon and the sky was still bathed in its scarlet light, which made blood out of the sea and tinted the sails a deceptively charming pink. Mike knew that Horace had forgotten to move his time. He spoke of it to his sailing-master in a lull, but this fellow found nothing strange about it!

And then, suddenly, the sun leaped up the sky and in the blink of an eye was at the zenith!

The sailing-master didn't think that was odd, either.

When Mike pointed out to Trombo that there were nearly as many English ships left in action as there had been at the beginning, even though half the English fleet had been sunk, Trombo shrugged and muttered something about the will of God.

Ranging back and forth and nipping at the heels of the English, driving them downwind to Nombre de Dios, the Spaniards seemed to be enjoying themselves. There seemed to be only one thought in the buccaneering fleet and that was to get away from the horrible punishment which kept searching their decks.

They seemed to be quite blind that they were coursing down upon a mighty shore battery.

At last the coast lost its blue cast and became green and filled with definite markings, and the harbor of Nombre de Dios opened its mouth to them. And like a host of shepherds running sheep, the Spanish forced in the wings and made the English spear towards that harbor. And like quaking sheep the English let themselves be herded.

Mike kept telling himself that there was something wrong with this victory. But maybe Horace had had a stroke—he hoped.

And then the foremost buccaneer, astonishingly enough the *Fleetfoot*, came into range of the Spanish forts. And swiftly narrowed the mile of blue waves to a gap a quarter of that.

And nothing happened.

Mike bawled to his signalmen and up rushed flags to break angrily, commanding the shore batteries to wake up and fire. Half the buccaneer fleet was in range now and, as the seconds raced by, finally was all within.

And still the forts did not fire.

"Treason!" howled Mike. "Trombo! Run that hoist again!"

Evidently the commander of the fort was not at all interested in Mike's signals.

Still, Mike told himself to cool himself down; it was not such a task to cut these English up, anyway, with just his fleet. They were so badly wrecked that they could not do much in return.

He shouted for hoists to order his fleet to close in.

Not until then did Mike get an inkling of what had happened to them. They were speeding up on the English which were in the shoals just off the forts. And the forts opened fire! But not on the English.

A hurricane of smoking hot iron crashed out at the Spanish fleet, and in one blast sent masts tottering and magazines exploding and men falling by the regiment!

178

Stunned inactivity descended upon the Spanish. Half a dozen ships broached to and lay there broadside, perfect targets as their sails shivered helplessly.

The forts thundered again and again.

The Spaniards struggled to beat up out of the shoal waters where the lighter-draft Englishmen had run. On every side the flaming ruins of tall galleons struck rocks. The sea was alive with the swimming men and a-glitter with the metal of scattered spars.

Suddenly the wind increased in force, and those which had struggled free on their six-point tacks now made so much leeway that they were again within range of the butchering forts.

Orders were nothing. The *Josef y Maria* clawed to windward while English ships, sailing, incredibly, much closer and faster, rushed out like wolfhounds to hang on her and rake her decks with flame. In seconds she was a smoking shambles, and a buccaneer to either side was casting grapnels over her gunwales to lay her aboard.

Cutlasses were making quick work of her boarding nets and now came to her decks a howling flood of half-clothed demons to sweep her shattered defenders forward and thence over her bows into the sea.

Across a deck carpeted with the blood of Spaniards and decorated with dismembered corpses came a hurricane of a man—Bristol!

Rapier in fist, battle lust distorting his face, the English captain leaped up the sterncastle gangway, shouting his battle cry.

Mike stood amid the ruins of his quarterdeck and toppled mizzen and beheld the devil swoop upon him. This, then, was the end. This was the part where Bristol ran him through for a dirty spick and fed his corpse to the sharks. And this was not cardboard scenery or puppet men. Pain and death were real!

Knowing well that he was doomed without trial, Mike acted without a glance at the rules. He sprang back without drawing his rapier, for he knew destiny meant death with that. A small serpentine which had been swiveled about to sweep the waist, but whose crew had died in the act without firing it, was pointed at Bristol. The linstock lay sizzling upon the planking. Mike scooped it up and slapped the touchhole. The huff singed his hand and then there was a white-hot flash!

Bristol was wreathed in smoke, untouched even by powder sparks.

Mike was struggling in the sea, swept away towards the shore by the spar which he had grasped. And in his battered ears rang the English cheer which meant victory, and the whir of a contented typewriter in the sky.

# CHAPTER
# THIRTEEN

It was nearly midnight when Mike, cast up again by the sea but only because of his own endeavor, gained the wooded heights above Nombre de Dios. He had struggled across the battlefield behind the forts, thus answering the riddle of the treachery. Bristol had landed a force to take them from the unfortified rear while the Spanish fleet was sucked into the trap from the sea.

There was no typewriter clattering now. There was nothing but the hot, sultry wind in the palms to remind him of it. The sullen sky was low upon Nombre de Dios and the smoldering ruins of the sacked city added their greasy thickness to the night.

It was the end, that was certain.

It was all over, though the English vessels still stood there in the roadstead, swinging at their cables while their crews debauched themselves. The story for Mike was done!

But Mike, weary and wounded, with no magic words to heal his hurts or his exhaustion, was not content. He had for one space changed that plot. And now there was no typewriter in the sky.

He had been created a swordsman without peer, a military genius, a clever and even treacherous gentleman. That had not been taken away.

Trombo was dead. They were all dead. But here was Mike, dragging himself through the tangle of wood towards the night-shrouded house which had so long been his home.

The windows showed lights behind their blinds as he crept by them, but he had not come here to peep through cracks and skulk. His rapier was at his side and no matter how tired was his arm—

He stepped up to the porch and found a buccaneer sentry sprawled there, left to guard but now very drunk. Mike pulled a pistol from the fellow's sash and holding the weapon in his left hand and keeping his sword in his right, kicked open the front door.

The table was very beautiful, lit by tall yellow candles whose soft beams fell upon Mike's crystal and gold. At one end sat the Lady Marion, painfully beautiful, smiling still though now she looked towards the door.

Bristol, silk-shirted and gold-sashed, started to his feet, the candlelight still in his eyes.

"Gog's wounds! Who's this?"

"I'm Mike de Wolf. The fellow you call Miguel St. Raoul de Lobo. Can it be," he added with sarcasm which had become habitual, "that I am not welcome in my own house?"

"Damme!" said Bristol. "Ye're a ghost!"

"No, m' lad," said Mike. "It's you that are a ghost!"

Lady Marion was white as she looked from Mike to Bristol.

"But ye're dead!" cried Bristol. "With my own eyes I saw it!"

"You've got the same eyes now," said Mike.

"But why—have you come back?" said Bristol.

"To kill you," said Mike.

It had no great effect upon Bristol. He had led a charmed life for so long that he was afraid of nothing. He reached towards his rapier which lay on the arms of a chair beside the wall.

Mike ached to drill him with the pistol but he knew the effect it would have upon the Lady Marion. He was too weary and starved to duel and he did not intend to give Bristol, who had had all the breaks, any others.

"Maybe you English fight before your women," said Mike. "I don't. There's light on the porch."

Bristol snorted in derision. "Marion, please pardon me while I kill this gentleman once and for all." And he strode past Mike, through the door and to the porch.

Mike shut the door behind himself and stood there for a moment looking at the English hero.

"You found her very glad to see you, I've no doubt," said Mike, humanly prey to jealousy.

"Aye," said Bristol. "And I've a debt to pay you, you hound, for sullying her fair name."

"It's not so sullied but what you asked her to marry you," said Mike.

"So I did," said Bristol.

"And she accepted," said Mike, "and then, amid a very touching scene, she said she could see you marching in triumph through the streets of London with your name on every lip and that at last she had found a man brave enough to command her humbleness and that she would be content to spend the remainder of her life worshipping you. And then she kissed you."

"Of course," said Bristol. "But—how did you know?"

"There's a lot I know."

"I hope you know I do you favor to fight you. I've a town full of my men—"

"All drunk," said Mike, glancing down the hill at the burning, raped wreck of the city. "And it's no favor."

Bristol shrugged. He had been pulling off his boots the better to grip the floor with his feet.

"I fear," said Mike, "that you'll never live to spend the millions in bullion you found here today. For, Tom Bristol, I intend to run you through."

"Guard!" cried Bristol.

Their blades crossed and with furious attack and defense they went at each other.

Mike thought the fury of Bristol's attack was the cause of the floor's shaking. He thought the way the lantern jiggled was done by a wild thrust. And he thought the roaring in his ears was in his head, an aftermath of cannon fire.

But it wasn't.

The shaking was soon so violent that it threw both of them down. Bristol, cursing, struggled up and was again thrown. Mike saw the porch roof start to come down and scurried back.

Lightning flashed down the sky, bluely lighting the woods where trees were falling. Thunder, by its very sound, seemed capable of tearing Mike apart. The porch came down and Bristol and the sleeping buccaneer were devoured in its shambles.

A frightened voice was crying from within the house, and then the Lady Marion was at the door, striving to force away the beam which blocked her egress. Again the lightning flared and the rain slashed furiously down.

Mike seized the Lady Marion's wrist and pulled her through the opening.

"What's happening?" she wept in terror.

"Come with me," said Mike, running down the path.

Again the lightning wiped out the blackness for a space and again the thunder rolled angrily over the sky. The wind was swiftly increasing in force and the rain was hammering painfully upon Mike's bare face. The earth shook and cast them down.

Through the water Mike reached for the Lady Marion and clutched her to him. It was impossible to stand. The flaring in the sky showed her scared face close to his.

"What is it?" she cried out to him.

"An earthquake and a storm," said Mike. "Nothing more."

"Where is Bristol?"

"He's dead," said Mike. "I didn't kill him. He was hit by the beams and buried when the porch fell."

"He's dead!"

"Yes. Marion, look at me. Have you no memory of loving me? Have you no thought of all the months we were together? You were happy with me—"

"Mike! Hold me! Hold me, Mike! I'm frightened!"

He held her close to him.

Lightning flashed so close by that Mike felt its concussion. And then, looking up against the whitened sky, he saw the huge black limbs and trunk of a tree come hurtling down at them.

He clutched Marion, trying to protect her body with his own. The earth shook and then vanished. The lightning cracked and snarled and then rain and earth and sky and wind, all these were gone.

And Mike's arms were empty.

# CHAPTER FOURTEEN

"You okay, buddy?" said the taxi driver. "You better let me take you home."

Mike looked wonderingly at the fellow, at the cab, at the dark street, quiet at this hour. "If it's dough, you c'n pay me when you got it. But you shouldn't be lying here. Somebody'll clip you."

Mike got up with help. "I'm all right," he muttered.

"You don't smell like ye're loopy," said the cabby. "You been sick or something?"

"Yeah," said Mike. "Yeah, I been sick." He steadied himself against the lamppost. "I'll be all right in a minute." He looked dazedly at the cab's license plates and finally it came home to him that they were those of the same year he had departed. It took him some little time to get it through his mind that he was back, alive and evidently safe.

"What's the name of this town?" said Mike.

"N'Yawk," said the cabby.

Mike felt relieved. He had come back, then.

"You sure you'll be all right?"

"Yeah. I feel fine now," said Mike.

"And you won't lemme take you home?"

"No. I'll walk a little way if you don't mind."

"Okay, you're the boss," said the cabby, getting into his hack and driving away.

Mike stood there for a long time, getting himself adjusted to the strangeness of being home again. In a way it was swell to be back. He'd get his fingers in shape and take another crack at the Philharmonic. And he'd see René and Kurt and Win Colt and Horace—

It would be so funny seeing Horace Hackett. Would it be possible, he wondered, ever to tell Horace about all this? In a way he should, just so he'd never be put into a story again—but again he shouldn't, because then Horace Hackett's already gigantic opinion of himself would probably expand beyond endurable limits. Horace was always talking about the powers of an author.

Mike essayed a walk and found that his faintness was gone. He slouched along the street, hands in the pockets of his sports jacket, chin on chest.

He had tried not to think about it and he tried now once more. But he knew. He had lost her. He would never see her again, for she was not of this world, and the other—maybe it did not even exist now. He had lost her, the only woman he would ever love. And though he tried not to, he could still feel her sobbing against him, knowing somehow that it was all over and done and that she was dead. He would never forget that—He stopped and braced himself against a wall.

"Move along, buddy," said a cop.

Mike moved along.

To find her—in a story. And now she would never be again.

He threw it off with bitterness. He was angry now. Angry with Horace Hackett, angry with this world and that other. Angry with the fate which had been handed him—

Ah, yes. The fate. It was his luck to meet somebody in a story and then return without her. It was his luck. But you couldn't expect the breaks all the time. You couldn't ask luck to run your way forever. He had had her for a little while, in a land ruled by a typewriter in the clouds. And now he was out of that and there was no type—

Abruptly Mike de Wolf stopped. His jaw slacked a trifle and his hand went up to his mouth to cover it. His eyes were fixed upon the fleecy clouds which scurried across the moon.

Up there—

God?

In a dirty bathrobe?

# ABOUT THE AUTHOR

Born in 1911, the son of a U.S. Naval officer, L. Ron Hubbard was raised in the state of Montana when it was still part of the great American frontier. He was early acquainted with the rugged outdoor life and as a boy earned the trust of the Blackfeet Indians who initiated him as a blood brother. He became the nation's youngest Eagle Scout at the age of thirteen.

During his teens, L. Ron Hubbard made several trips to Asia, carefully recording his observations and experiences in a series of diaries, as well as noting down story ideas resulting from his many adventures. His travels were extensive, including Malaysia, Indonesia, the ports of India and the Western Hills of China. By the time he was 19, he had logged over a quarter of a million miles on land and sea in an era well before commercial air travel.

Returning to the United States, he enrolled at The George Washington University where he studied engineering and participated in the first classes on atomic and molecular phenomena. He was also an award-winning contributor to the University's literary magazine.

While still a student, he took up "barnstorming." He quickly gained a reputation as a daring and skilled pilot of both gliders and motorized planes and became a frequent correspondent for *The Sportsman's Pilot*.

His intense interest in understanding the nature of man and the different races and cultures of the world took him once again to the high seas in 1933. This time he led two expeditions through the Caribbean. He was subsequently awarded membership in the prestigious Explorers' Club and would carry their flag on three more expeditions.

Drawing from his travels and first-hand adventures, L. Ron Hubbard began his professional writing career in 1933. He went on to create an amazing wealth of stories in a variety of genres which included adventure, mystery, detective and western, producing a broad catalog of entertainment which attracted a huge readership. In 1935, at age 25, he was elected president of the New York Chapter of the American Fiction Guild. During his tenure as president, the Fiction Guild membership included many renowned authors such as Raymond Chandler, Dashiell Hammett, Edgar Rice Burroughs and other notables who were the life-blood of the American literary marketplace.

Mr. Hubbard was invited to Hollywood in 1937, where he wrote the story and scripted fifteen screenplays for Columbia's box office serial hit "The Secret of Treasure Island." While in Hollywood, he also worked on screenplays and story plots for other wide-screen productions.

In 1938, fully established and recognized as one of the country's top-selling authors, he was approached by the publishers of *Astounding Science Fiction* magazine to write for them. They believed that in order to significantly increase the circulation of their speculative fiction magazines, they would need to feature real people in their stories. L. Ron Hubbard was the one writer they knew who could deliver this better than any other. The upshot was a wealth of celebrated science fiction and fantasy stories, which not only expanded the scope of these genres, but established Mr. Hubbard as one of the founding fathers of the great "Golden Age of Science Fiction."

His initial works of science fiction captured the hearts and minds of readers and he soon started writing fantasy stories as well, with the publication of "The Ultimate Adventure" in April 1939, in *Astounding*'s sister publication, *Unknown.*

By mid-1940, L. Ron Hubbard had published the classic tale "Final Blackout," a gripping novel of unending war. "Not half a dozen stories in the history of science-fiction can equal the grim power of this novel . . ." stated *Astounding*'s editor, John W. Campbell, Jr. Immediately following this, his story "Fear" appeared, setting a whole new standard for horror fiction and influencing generations of writers. Stephen King calls "Fear" a true classic of "creeping, surreal menace and horror." He completed that incredibly productive year with the publication of "Typewriter in the Sky" in the November and December issues of *Unknown.*

With the advent of World War II, L. Ron Hubbard was called to active duty as an officer in the U.S. Navy. It was not until 1947 that he was once again turning out exciting stories for his many fans. These included the benchmark novel "To the Stars"—a powerful work centering on the impact of space travel at light-speed—and his critically acclaimed story, "The End Is Not Yet." It was during this same period that he wrote the ever-popular "Ole Doc Methuselah" stories. Published under the pen name René Lafayette, a byline which L. Ron Hubbard reserved for the series, the adventures of Ole Doc and his companion Hippocrates quickly became a reader favorite.

In 1950, with the culmination of years of research on the subject of the mind resulting in the publication of "Dianetics: The Modern Science of Mental Health," L. Ron Hubbard left the field of fiction and for the next three decades, he dedicated his life to writing and publishing millions of words of non-fiction concerning the nature of man and the betterment of the human condition.

However, in 1982, to celebrate his 50th anniversary as a professional author, L. Ron Hubbard returned to science fiction and released his giant blockbuster, "Battlefield Earth," the biggest science fiction book ever written. "Battlefield Earth" became an international bestseller with millions of copies sold in over 60 countries. In the U.S. alone, it appeared on national bestseller lists for over 32 weeks.

He followed this with an even more spectacular achievement, his magnum opus—the ten-volume MISSION EARTH®

series, every one of which became a *New York Times* bestseller. "Mission Earth" is not only a grand science fiction adventure in itself, but in the best tradition of Jonathan Swift and Lewis Carroll, is a rollicking satirical romp through the foibles and fallacies of our civilization.

L. Ron Hubbard departed this life on January 24, 1986. His prodigious and creative output over more than half a century as a professional author is a true publishing phenomenon. To date, his books have been published in over 100 countries and 31 languages, resulting in over 116 million copies of his works sold around the world. This vast library includes over 230 popular fiction novels, novelettes and short stories (all of which are planned to be republished in the years to come) as well as hundreds of non-fiction publications, establishing L. Ron Hubbard as one of the most acclaimed and widely read authors of all time.

# "I am Always Happy to Hear from my Readers."

These were the words of L. Ron Hubbard, who was always very interested in hearing from his friends and readers. He made a point of staying in communication with everyone he came in contact with over his fifty-year career as a professional writer, and he had thousands of fans and friends that he corresponded with all over the world.

The publishers of L. Ron Hubbard's literary works wish to continue this tradition and would very much welcome letters and comments from you, his readers, both old and new.

Any message addressed to Author's Affairs Director at Bridge Publications will be given prompt and full attention.

BRIDGE PUBLICATIONS, INC.
4751 Fountain Avenue
Los Angeles, California 90029